SMOKE DETECTOR

Eric Wright

SMOKE DETECTOR
An Inspector Charlie Salter Novel

G.K.HALL &CO.
Boston, Massachusetts
1985

Published by G. K. Hall & Co.
A publishing subsidiary of ITT

Published in Large Print by arrangement
with Charles Scribner's Sons.

G. K. Hall Large Print Book Series.

Set in 16pt Plantin.

Library of Congress Cataloging in Publication Data

Wright, Eric.
  Smoke detector.

  (G. K. Hall large print book series)
  1. Large type books. I. Title.
[PR9199.3.W66S6 1985]   813'.54   84–29053
ISBN 0–8161–3900–8 (lg. print)

Grateful thanks are due to
the Stuart Jackson Gallery of Yorkville
for their help and advice.

For Tory and Jessica

SMOKE DETECTOR

CHAPTER ONE

September is Toronto's best month. The summer can be hot and sticky, and winter goes on too long, but for a few weeks between the two seasons the city is blessed with warm, dry, sunny days and nights cool enough to sleep.

Salter opened his eyes and looked at the bit of sky framed by the small third-floor window: white branches of a silver birch dressed in yellow leaves, all set against a clear blue sky. He rummaged under the duvet in search of his wife and squeezed her awake. 'Look,' he said. 'Look outside.'

He slid out of bed and crossed to the window, naked and bent-kneed, keeping his bottom half out of sight of all the neighbours who might be watching through binoculars. 'Bloody marvellous,' he said. Then, slightly chilled, he crawled back into bed and reached for Annie, but she had disappeared while he was drinking in the morning. He heard her turn on the shower one floor below and he lay still for five minutes until the noise of running water stopped. Then he ran down the stairs and pounded on the bathroom

1

door. Annie let him in and locked the door behind him, and Salter sat on the edge of the tub and watched her dry herself. It was his favourite way of starting the day.

She was forty, and as far as he could tell she had not changed a wrinkle in the eighteen years since he had first seen her naked. She often pointed out marks of decrepitude on her aging, sagging epidermis, but all the flaws she showed him looked no more than the tucks and rumples that were unavoidable when a human skin was stretched over such a complicated frame. Salter felt a grumbling in his loins as she shrouded herself in a bathtowel. He sighed and turned on the shower.

At breakfast, which they ate while their two sons were getting ready for school, Annie said, 'By the way, there are some things I have to tell you, but finish eating first.'

Salter's euphoria ebbed away. 'By the way' delivered on a descending scale, with a heavy pause after 'way', was bad news, always. He ate two pieces of toast and looked at the paper. Something fairly substantial was coming, he guessed, or Annie would have delivered herself of it immediately. The boys left separately, eleven-year-old Seth first, with a kiss, then his fourteen-year-old brother, Angus, without even a goodbye. Odd, that. Angus had stopped kissing people some months before, but he usually said something by way of an exit.

'Is it Angus?' Salter asked, when they were alone.

'I might as well start with him,' she said.

Christ! There was a *list*.

Annie disappeared upstairs and returned with two magazines which she put beside his plate. He picked up the first one gingerly and opened it at random. A photograph ran across two pages, a picture of a naked girl with enormous breasts kneeling over a recumbent male. Salter picked up the other one. It was devoted to group activities.

'Where did you find these?' he asked.

'In Angus's cupboard.'

'Put them back.'

'*Put them back?*'

'Right. Where you found them.'

'What are you going to do?'

'Me? I don't know. But if you put them back I'll have time to think.'

'I've already told him I found them.'

'Shit. All right. So. One: Angus has been reading skin magazines. What else?'

'The nurse phoned yesterday. I forgot to tell you. They want you to take some more tests.'

Salter had recently undergone his annual medical and been pronounced fit. 'Why? What for?' he asked.

'It's something to do with your urine.'

Salter's voice became noisy from fear. 'What? What is? What did she say? I've got diabetes?'

Annie shook her head. 'She said there was blood in it.'

'Blood? What does that mean? How long have I got?'

'She said it is probably nothing. But she's fixed an appointment for you to see a specialist today.'

'What's the rush? I thought it took six months to get an appointment with a specialist.'

'You got lucky. This one has a cancellation.'

'What kind of specialist?' Salter's mind raced over all the fatal diseases that strike middle-aged policemen.

'I think she said urologist.'

'A piss-artist?' He laughed in spite of the scenes that were rushing through his head. Had he made a will? 'That's it, then? Angus is feeling his oats and I'm dying. Anything else?'

4

'I will be working late for a few days. Maybe a couple of weeks.'

'Doing what?'

'We're very busy, Charlie, and you just don't turn down new accounts these days.' Annie was a 'gofer' in an advertising agency; she arranged the locations, the sets and the props for filming commercials.

'Okay,' he said. 'Angus is a sex maniac. I'm dying. You're leaving home. Anything else?'

'You are such a help, Charlie. I'm sorry you're worried about the doctor, but I'm sure you're all right. Don't take it out on me.'

'Anything *else?*'

'Yes. The screen door has jumped off its track on the third floor. One of the wheels seems to be broken.'

'I'll look at it tonight.'

In many ways it was the worst news of all, because it was probably the beginning of a month-long saga in which he spent every Saturday morning and some part of the week trying to understand the trouble, locating a hardware store which still sold the replacement part (the door was ten years old), and finally, learning from scratch, by trial and error, how to replace the wheel without any of the tools that the job required. Salter

5

fixed what he could about the house, but he had no mechanical ability, and confronted with a new problem for which there was no standard repairman, he anticipated the ultimate failure of his efforts from the beginning and tackled the job in a temper. He had also lost interest in the house, having reached the age when he preferred to spend his time in the present rather than repairing for the future. The years were passing quickly, and Salter had lost any desire to putter. He got up to go.

'Think about Angus, won't you, Charlie?' Annie asked again.

Salter put on his jacket. 'I'll think about him, and me, and the third-floor screen,' he said. 'How late will you be?'

'If I'm going to be after seven, I'll call you.' Annie got up and opened the refrigerator door. 'There's bacon and eggs, cold roast beef, half an apple pie, cheese, and a cupboard full of canned soup. You can manage.' She put her arms around him in a gesture that was meant to be friendly, comforting and sexy, designed to take care of all his worries.

But as he walked to the subway, the perfect morning weather now seemed an ironic backdrop to his own threatened cosmos.

6

At the office, Sergeant Gatenby greeted him like an old nanny who knows of a treat in store for her favourite child. Gatenby was not much older than Salter, but he was known as The Oldest Sergeant in the Force because of his white hair and avuncular manner, both of which he had acquired in his thirties. In those days he was known as The Oldest Constable in the Force, and most of his career had been spent performing all those duties which called for a kindly old copper to represent the Force to the public, especially to children.

'Chiefie wants to see you,' he said now. 'I think he's got a job for us.' 'Chiefie' was Staff Superintendent Orliff. As the result of emerging on the losing side of a recent political struggle within the Force, Salter had been an outsider for a year. Then, through a piece of luck, one of the odd jobs he was given provided a chance to solve a homicide case in Montreal, earning him the gratitude of the Montreal police, and thus of his own bosses. He had been let know then that his period of exile could be coming to an end, and also that he had been exaggerating the depth of the hostility to him. 'No one,' Orliff, his new superintendent, had said, 'holds grudges for ever.'

Salter went now to Orliff's office where the

Superintendent was waiting.

'Arson and homicide,' Orliff said, tapping the corners of the pile of paper in front of him to make the edges square. His desk was immaculately tidy, and along its outer edge was a row of neat stacks of paper like the one under his hand.

'I'm on the Arson Squad?' Salter asked.

'You're helping out. The squad has its hands full—these things come in bunches and there isn't anyone to spare. That Jamaican case is keeping everyone busy,' Orliff said, referring to a manhunt currently on for the killer of a young black girl who had been raped and murdered on her way home from babysitting. The black community was demanding action.

'What's the story?'

'An antique dealer on Bloor West. Store caught fire last night. The fire department saved the building, but they found the owner dead. Smoke inhalation, probably, but the autopsy will show. The fire started in the basement and the Fire Marshal thinks someone put a torch to the place. The owner has an apartment above the store, although he didn't live there. He had a home on—' Orliff checked his notes—'Albany Avenue, in the neighbourhood. I guess he used the

8

apartment sometimes, because he had a bed up there, and some clothes. That's it. You'd better talk to the Marshal's office first, and then go and see what you think.'

'Has the Fire Marshal finished? I thought those boys did their own investigations.'

'Only the arson side. As I said, this is homicide. The coroner has it now and he's told us to get going. The fire was no accident, so the death is homicide by person or persons unknown, as they say.'

'What am I doing? Just filling in until Homicide can spare someone?'

'That's right, Charlie. They'll take over when they can, but you might have it cleaned up by then.' Orliff smiled. 'I told them you were busy on a couple of other assignments but that if they were desperate you would have a look at it. They said they'd like you to do that.' Orliff watched Salter, and waited. He was making two points: first, he, Orliff, was looking after Salter to the extent of making him seem busy, and, second, that Homicide still wanted Salter to help out after they had heard who he was. Together they added up to a significant small improvement in Salter's status. If he turned the assignment down, which he probably could, he might wait a long time for another one.

'Who is over there now?' he asked.

'Constable Katesmark is guarding it. Here's the report from the officer who got to the fire first. And here's the name of the investigator from the Fire Marshal's office. Lotsa luck, Charlie.'

Salter took the sheet of paper which Orliff had prepared and watched the Superintendent make a note to himself that the case was assigned to Salter, with the date and a time. The Superintendent had risen steadily through the ranks chiefly by being careful, and one of his habits was to make a record of everything. Thus by the time a case was in its second day, Orliff had a pile of reports, memos, and notes to himself, recording, literally, everything that had been said and done. These cases he laid in a row around the edge of his desk. On the shelves behind him there were another thirty or more that were not quite dead; in the filing cabinets were dozens more that were finished, but Orliff was not yet ready to put into deep storage. Among the neat stacks were several personal projects: one of them was the Superintendent's continuing investigation into various annuity schemes; another contained the plans for the cottage he was building in the Kawartha hills. The object of working, for Orliff, was to provide for the good life, and he kept his work and its object in front of him all the time.

Salter went back to his office and told Gatenby what was up. 'First murder, now arson—they'll be giving us espionage stuff soon,' Gatenby said, chuckling. 'Charlie Salter, Special Agent. Ha, ha, ha. Anything for me to do yet?'

'Not yet, Frank. Just tell anyone who needs me that I'm busy, on a case.' Salter permitted himself a small smile. The day was improving slightly.

'Oh, I'll tell them.' Gatenby picked up Salter's IN tray. 'I'll tell them. I'll get rid of this first.' He sat down and began referring the assignments one by one back to the sender.

★   ★   ★

Salter started by reading the police report. The alarm had been phoned in at 1.53 a.m. The police and the fire trucks had arrived together, the report said. The fire was confined to the basement and very quickly extinguished. The owner, who was found at the foot of the stairs leading up to the second floor, was pronounced dead on arrival at the

11

hospital.

Salter phoned the Fire Marshal's office and spoke to the investigator, asking the obvious question first. Could it have been an accident?

'We don't think so. The agent used was gasoline, or something equally volatile—the guys on the truck said they could smell it when they arrived. And there was no container around, which means that someone poured gasoline on the basement floor, lit it and got out right away.'

'Spontaneous combustion?' Salter asked. The question was probably foolish, but he knew Orliff would ask *him*.

'That's something else. Usually it involves something like linseed oil. Look, Inspector, I'm just going to bed. I pass the fire on my way home, or I can do. Why don't you meet me there and I'll take you over it? You're new to this, aren't you? Usually it's Munnings or Hutter on these jobs.' The investigator's voice was friendly, but weary.

'That's right, I am. I'd be glad of any help.'

'Half an hour then. See you there.'

Salter hung up and shoved the report in his pocket. 'I've gone to the fire, Frank,' he said, standing up. 'I'll be back at noon.'

Bloor Street, which once marked the northern boundary of the city, is now a continuous shopping district running through the heart of Toronto. In the centre, where it intersects with Yonge Street, the stores are fashionable and expensive, but within a few blocks in either direction the character changes as the street becomes the 'Main Street' of the local district, changing continuously with the economic and racial character of the area.

The building that Salter was looking for was several blocks west of Bathurst Street, on the far side of a district dominated by Honest Ed's, a giant bargain mart decorated like a cross between a circus and an amusement arcade, covered in coloured lights and hung with revolving balls, a discount store that attracts huge crowds with daily specials like chickens at one cent each (limit one per customer). Partly through the benevolent whim of the proprietor of this establishment, Markham Street, which crosses Bloor just west of Honest Ed's, has developed into a little colony of artists' studios, restaurants, and second-hand dealers, which the chief

13

landlord calls 'Mirvish Village'.

At this point, Bloor Street is a pleasant muddle of small stores and restaurants, housed in the same two- and three-storey buildings that were erected in the early years of the century when the district was largely Anglo-Saxon. The mix of races has changed, but the street still looks, as Salter's mother had once said out of her girlhood memories of South London, like Toronto's Tooting Broadway, crowded with small clothing stores and greengrocers. Now the travel agents have signs in Greek and Portuguese, and mangoes and red bananas sell as briskly as carrots and Brussels sprouts. Pasta is on sale everywhere, a staple not only of the Italians, but also of the large population of students who live nearby, within walking distance of the University of Toronto, which sprawls hugely across the city to the south-east.

Salter found a parking space a block away from the fire and walked back to the store. The name was still discernible: 'THE BOTTOM DRAWER—ANTIQUES AND COLLECTIBLES (C. DRECKER).' The front of the store was boarded with plywood, but the door was open and a policeman stood on guard talking to a grey-haired man about Salter's age.

Salter produced his identification, and the other man put out his hand. 'I'm the guy you were talking to,' he said. 'Hayes, Fire Marshal's office.'

He was heavily built without fat, not dramatically dirty, but as Salter got close he could see the line of ash around his boots and the soot in the creases of the man's face that told of a long night's work. His exhaustion was evident in the slump of his body. 'We'd better go inside,' he said, in a voice that also said to Salter that it was long after closing time but he would do what was necessary to fill the policeman in.

'Started in the basement,' Hayes said. 'Want to go down?'

Salter nodded and Hayes switched on the electric lantern he was carrying. 'There's no power, of course,' he said. He led the way through to the back of the store, down a flight of steps to the dark hole below, and shone his lantern around. The room was charred and blackened and still dripping with the water that had been poured into it. Surprisingly, the fire seemed to have burnt only a small part of the ceiling, making a hole about six feet across at the back of the basement opposite the stairs.

'They got here in time to save it,' the
15

investigator said. 'It didn't take much to put it out. The damage is mostly smoke.'

And water, thought Salter, looking at the sodden mess. 'What makes you think it was arson?' he asked.

'Okay,' Hayes said, and cleared his throat. When he spoke again he assumed a formal, pedagogical tone. 'The firemen smelled gasoline, or something like it. The fire started on the floor. Look. See this patch?' He pointed to a bare patch on the concrete floor. 'Nothing to burn there, but something burnt *on* it if you get me. Now. The fire took off over here.' He pointed to a charred mess underneath the burnt part of the ceiling. 'My guess is that that was a pile of rags, probably soaked in oil. There's not much else to burn down here. He didn't use it for storage. So you've got a gasoline fire which turned into an oil fire. That's why there was so much smoke.'

'But it couldn't have been spontaneous?'

'You don't mean spontaneous,' Hayes said. 'You mean could it have been sparked by something accidentally, right?'

Salter nodded.

'First,' Hayes continued, 'there's no furnace. The whole place is electric—lighting, heating, hot water—the lot. The

16

wiring runs round the ceiling, see. Now you do get a gasoline fire set off by an electric spark—any kind of spark will do—but you've got to have the right mixture of gas and air up at the ceiling level, you follow me? Okay. Now, if you get that mixture you also get one hell of an explosion—it would take the roof off. But there was no explosion. I talked to some of the locals who were gawking and no one even heard a woomp. So the gas ignited almost as soon as it was poured. That is, somebody poured gas around, lit it right away, and got the hell out. Even a couple of minutes would have been dangerous. Another thing, there was no container. We didn't find a can or anything else in the basement that could have held the gas. Whoever poured it took the can with him.'

Salter looked around the basement, following the investigator's argument. The floor had obviously not been swept for years. There were several iron coat hangers, dozens of nails, pieces of wire, hooks and broken hinges forming a kind of metal rubble all over the floor, but nothing that could have contained gasoline. He pointed to a light-bulb. 'What happened to that?' he asked. 'I thought those things would just explode.' The bulb bulged distortedly on one side.

Hayes smiled. 'It's one of the ways you can tell the point of origin,' he said. 'This one is obvious, but if it wasn't the light-bulbs would tell you because they expand in the direction of the heat.'

'What about the windows?' Salter asked. There were two small windows at ground level, hinged on the top of the frame and opening upwards and inwards. The one farthest from the fire was still intact, the bolts rusted into place. The other window was close enough to the pile of rags to have been scorched. Hayes waited for his pupil to examine it for himself. At some time the glass had been broken and replaced with a cheap plastic storm window. The charred cardboard edging was still in place, but the plastic pane had melted and shrivelled away, and a fresh draught blew in through the gap. The frame, like its companion, was still bolted and rusted shut, and the cross-struts were still intact.

'No one came in there,' Salter conceded. 'What now?'

'Upstairs,' Hayes said, leading the way. 'What's your regular assignment?' he asked conversationally.

Who knows? thought Salter. He remembered Gatenby's joke. 'I'm on the

Intelligence detail,' he said. 'Counter-espionage mostly. Other stuff, too, though.' He smiled to show he was joking, but the investigator had his back to him and just nodded to show he had heard.

No more jokes, Salter told himself.

Hayes stopped at the foot of the stairs leading to the second floor. 'This is where we found him,' he said. 'He was in his shorts. There were no marks that I could see, but the pathologist will tell you about that. Smoke inhalation, pretty certainly.'

'Could he have set it himself?' Salter asked, and regretted it immediately.

'You think he might have set fire to the basement and gone upstairs to have a lie-down?' Hayes's voice was tinged with wonder. Then his weariness took over as he explained to this incompetent they had sent (instead of Munnings or Hutter) the stupidity of his question.

Salter cut in. 'Look, I'm sorry. I'm not on the regular arson detail. I need a refresher course, so I would be grateful for a step-by-step account of how you came to your conclusions. Okay? You're the expert, so tell me.'

Thus appealed to, the investigator softened slightly. 'It's been a hairy three days,' he

19

said. 'Last weekend there were fifty-eight fires in Metro. The average for a weekend is about thirty.'

'No wonder you're tired,' Salter said. 'So,' he continued, 'you found the owner here, in his underwear. If, by some kind of magic, he *had* set the fire, there would be a can around. Then I would also have to figure out why he got undressed to set fire to his own store. Right? But the obvious thing is that he was overcome by smoke. Right?'

Hayes nodded. 'That's about it,' he said. 'Let's look at the rest of it, upstairs.' He turned to lead the way.

At the top of the stairs to the second floor a small landing gave access to a tiny apartment. At the back a newly renovated bathroom looked over the yard, which was no more than a parking space for a blue Volkswagen truck. Next to the bathroom, a small bedroom had been used for a workroom, and contained the dismantled pieces of a table and a rocking-chair. There was a kitchen next to the bedroom, and then a living-room which took up the front of the apartment and looked over the street. This room was furnished with a mixture of odds and ends from Drecker's stock: a double bed that opened out from a settee, two odd armchairs, and an old coffee table. The floor was covered with an oriental-looking rug, and a cocktail cabinet in blonde wood stood in the corner next to a television set that was angled so that it could be watched from the bed. There were no pictures on the walls, and the total effect was of a camp rather than of a room used for living. The damage here was negligible, although the room, like the whole house, stank of wet smoke.

'Funny way to live, isn't it?' Hayes said. 'No pictures or anything.'

'I don't think he lived here,' Salter said. He looked around the room. Beside the bed was a bottle of rum, about a quarter full, and a huge empty cola bottle.

'The pathologist will tell us,' Hayes said, 'but my guess is he was too drunk to help himself.'

Salter nodded. 'It makes sense, doesn't it? Let's go downstairs.'

The assortment of soaked and blackened furniture that had made up the stock was still arranged for sale in the store, although some of the shelves were empty.

'The insurance people took a look already,' the constable on guard said. 'Drecker's assistant went off with them. He said he'd be back as soon as he'd finished with the adjuster.'

I wonder what he had that was worth a buck, Salter thought, looking around. Even under the smoke it was easy to guess that Drecker did not aim very high. There was a cheap metal desk, a huge old typewriter, and a filing cabinet that looked as though someone had tried to kick the side in. The floor was bare, and the shelving had been assembled from a lot of old bookcases of different sizes.

'If that's it, I'm going home to bed,' Hayes said, breaking into Salter's thoughts.

'Yes, thanks. Thanks a lot,' Salter shook hands with the investigator. 'Can I call you if I need more help?' It was as much an apology for any irritation he had caused as a request for help.

'Sure,' Hayes said. 'But I guess Munnings or Hutter will be taking over soon, won't they? You can go back to catching spies.' He nodded and left.

No more jokes, Salter promised himself.

'He's got us mixed up with the mounties, I reckon, sir,' the constable said, grinning.

Salter looked at him, searching for the remark that would relieve his own feelings. In the end he said nothing, but the constable read his face accurately and turned away.

Salter looked at the man's back. Another enemy, he thought.

He bent down to look at the front door which the firemen had smashed off its hinges. There were two locks, but only one of them was secured. On the back door, which opened on to Drecker's parking space, both locks were in place. Did that mean anything? Salter came to two opposite and equally convincing conclusions, and set the problem aside. He walked out on to the street to scout for neighbours who might have seen something. The buildings on both sides of the street were all two-storey affairs. All of them had stores on the ground floor, while most of the second floors were occupied by insurance and travel agents. At the end of the block an old three-storey apartment building offered possibilities, but most of the tenants would be at work now. Checking the building was a job for others.

Salter returned to the store and nearly collided in the doorway with a young man who was also on his way in.

'Who are you?' Salter asked without preamble.

From inside, the constable answered. 'This is Dennis Nelson, the assistant.' He left Salter to introduce himself.

'Inspector Salter,' the policeman said. 'I would like some questions answered.'

'About me?' Nelson asked. He had bright ginger hair cut in an English style with a drooping lock over his forehead, and a thick fair moustache which hung in points around his mouth. His face was smooth and round like that of a grown-up cherub, with an expression of eagerness approaching glee, giving him the air of a schoolboy on a picnic. He was casually but carefully dressed in chino pants and a thick dark blue sweater. Salter judged his age at about twenty-two or -three.

'About everything here,' Salter said. 'You. Your boss. The regular customers—whatever you can tell me.'

Nelson looked around the blackened store. 'Could we go somewhere else?' he asked. 'I was just going to take the records home for safe-keeping until someone tells me what happens next. Why don't we talk in my apartment? It's not far from here.' He stood with his feet together and one arm pointed at right-angles in the direction of his apartment, somewhere down Bloor Street, giving the impression that at a nod from Salter he would give a little kick and launch himself horizontally sideways, to arrive in a trice at

24

the apartment.

Salter shrugged and nodded. A pixie was a nice change from an exhausted fire marshal and a wounded constable.

Nelson sprang across the room to a single-drawer filing cabinet that stood next to the cash register. 'Everything is in here,' he said. 'If you have a car we could load it in and drive over. I live on Washington Avenue.'

'What's in the cash register?'

'Nothing. There should be a float of twenty-five dollars here.' He dived under the counter and came up with a dirty envelope full of change and small bills, and held it high in the air, inquiringly. 'Everything else went into the night deposit box,' he said.

'Put the money in the filing cabinet,' Salter said. 'We'll take it with us. I'll get the car.'

When he returned, he double-parked with his engine running, and the two men loaded the filing cabinet into the back seat. The constable looked after the car doors and saluted carefully as they drove off.

'You'd better do a U-turn,' Nelson said. 'You can't go around the block because of the one-way street system.'

They turned east along Bloor, past Honest Ed's, to Spadina Avenue, and then south to Washington, the first street. Nelson lived in a house near the Spadina end of the street, and Salter drove the car up on to the sidewalk outside the house. They carried the filing cabinet into the kitchen and put it on one end of a long counter. Nelson twirled about with paper towels, cleaning the soot off the cabinet while Salter looked around the apartment. It was decorated in a style he faintly recognised, and Annie would identify when he got home: most of the colours were black and white, making the apartment look like the set of an old movie; the rug was white, the small piano was white, as well as the curtains, most of the wall-space and woodwork, and some of the furniture. In the centre of the room was a huge black glass coffee table, and one of the armchairs and a footstool were also black. The ornaments above the fireplace were made of frosted glass, except for a clock which advertised Sweet Caporal cigarettes and belonged in a bus station on the prairies, and another clock of white plastic with a tiny black Harold Lloyd dangling from the minute hand. On the walls were several drawings in black ink of people writhing, clipped between sheets of glass without frames; two whole walls were filled with bookshelves, crammed with books and magazines about art.

Nelson stood poised in the doorway of the kitchen. 'Coffee, Inspector?'

'All right.' Salter sat down, choosing the black armchair in case he had any soot on him. In a few minutes, Nelson reappeared, moving as if on roller-skates, bearing a Coca-Cola tray on which he carried two white mugs, a jug of cream, and a bowl of sugar. Salter sipped and found the coffee delicious.

'If you want to smoke, I have an ashtray somewhere,' Nelson said.

'No, thanks. Now, Mr Nelson, tell me first about your boss, C. Drecker. What does the "C" stand for?'

'Cyril. What do you want to know? I didn't like him,' Nelson said with a flourish of his cup, looking brightly at Salter to see if he had shocked him.

'I see. This is going to be easy, then. You went out last night and set fire to the store and killed him?'

'O no. I'm sorry he's dead—' here Nelson struck a pose personifying Sorrow— 'but only in a general way.' The smile returned.

'Why didn't you like him?'

'Because I saw him swindling people, and because he was abusive and flatulent.' Nelson was solemn now. His brightness was undiminished and he spoke without rancour,

27

but in a determined clear voice. 'Never speak evil of the dead, and all that, but if the police followed *that* rule you wouldn't get anywhere, would you?'

Salter took out his notebook. Nelson obviously felt free to express his dislike of Drecker without arousing Salter's curiosity, although he might have decided that the police were bound to find out about it, anyway.

'How was he abusive?' Salter asked.

'He made fun of me, or tried to. He was snide.'

'How?'

'He made fun of my lifestyle.'

Salter waved a hand around the room. 'All this?' he asked. 'Looks nice to me.' What was it? Apart from the Sweet Caporal clock and the Coca-Cola tray, everything in the room was black or white.

Nelson looked at Salter speculatively for a few moments. Then: 'Not my taste, Inspector,' he said. 'My sexual orientation.'

For a few seconds Salter was genuinely puzzled. Then he realized what he was being told. Feeling like a yokel, he decided to act like one, but a yokel without prejudices. 'You're queer, are you, Mr Nelson?' he asked, like someone enquiring, 'You're

28

Hindu, or vegetarian, or new to the district?'

'I'm bisexual, Inspector,' Nelson said, like a boy who could not tell a lie.

'Fine, fine. And Drecker made fun of this, did he? How?' Might as well beat the subject to death.

'He used to ask me if I fancied this or that male. And he would fantasize about what he would like to do to the women customers, aloud.'

'And what did you do?'

'When he went too far, I told him to stop. Mostly I ignored him. Once I asked him why he was so interested in the gay scene. That shut him up for a long time.'

'He doesn't sound very attractive, Mr Nelson. Dirty talker, dirty habits.' Salter pretended a bit more sympathy than he felt. Drecker sounded to him no worse than most of the men he knew, even if he had kept the locker-room talk going later in life than usual.

'Only around me, Inspector. Other people thought he was a fine fellow. Especially his girlfriends. They found him attractive, all right.'

'Girlfriends?'

'He always had one, sometimes two at the same time.'

29

'Was that what the upstairs apartment was all about?'

'Mostly,' Nelson nodded.

'So, he was a pig as far as you were concerned,' Salter said, again discounting something for Nelson's fastidiousness. 'Why did you work for him?'

'I wanted to learn about the Toronto dealer scene. I know something about antiques, and The Bottom Drawer was a place to pick up the economics of the trade. The worm's eye view of it, anyway. I hope to get my own shop eventually.'

'He was also a crook, you say. Enough of one to have enemies who would want to kill him?'

Nelson shook his head. 'I wouldn't have thought so. He wasn't that big—more of a chiseller, really. Drecker was always looking to buy for a dollar and sell for a hundred, always trying to get something for nothing.' Gradually, as Salter responded seriously to his words, Nelson was becoming less galvanic.

'Was he known for it?'

'In the trade, yes. The bigger dealers, the ones Drecker sometimes sold to, didn't trust him. They always demanded full provenance of everything he sold them.'

'They thought he might be a fence?'

'They knew he would be if there wasn't much risk.'

'Who are these dealers? Who did he do business with, say, in the last six months?'

Nelson pointed to the file cabinet. 'It's all in there,' he said. 'I could make up a list for you, but it would take a bit of time.'

'Tomorrow?'

'Sure.'

'Good. Next. Are you aware of anyone else who had a grudge against him? Any big arguments, that kind of thing?'

'There have been a couple of shouting matches, lately. One old lady sold him a harvest table for ten dollars. He had it cleaned up and put it out for six hundred.'

'You know her name?'

'No. Drecker dealt in cash when he could. No receipts for stuff like that. But that was two months ago. Then there was the guy who fixed the bathroom, Raymond Darling. Drecker must have tried to swindle him because he came back last week and they had a shouting match upstairs. He came back twice. I know him—he's a friend of a friend of mine. More coffee?'

Salter pushed his cup forward. 'Write his name down, will you?' he said, pointing to a little block of white notepaper that fitted into a perspex box on the coffee table. 'Along with where I could get hold of him. Now, one more question, Mr Nelson.'

'Where was I last night? Right?'

'Yes. Where were you last night?'

'I was here until one o'clock this morning, and then I left and spent the rest of the night with a friend.'

'A friend?'

'A friend,' confirmed Nelson. 'A *lady*,' he added. His face creased into a 'gotcha' smile.

'Her name?'

'Julia Costa. You want her address, of course.' He wrote it down on the same slip of paper and handed it to Salter.

'And until one o'clock you were here, alone?'

'No.' Nelson said. He was not smiling now. 'Until one o'clock I was here with the person I live with. We were having an argument and I couldn't stand it any longer so I got a cab and went over to Julia's.'

'I see. Your friend could confirm this?'

'Yes. Jake will be back this afternoon. Could I ask you a favour? Would you mind *not* telling Jake where I went when I left him?'

'All right. Why?'

32

Nelson put his hands in his pockets and pushed himself against the back of the chair. 'He's jealous,' he said. 'It's one of the things we quarrelled about. He wants to know where I am all the time, and I need some kind of private life of my own. I've got to have some air.'

It seemed his proper element.

'I see,' Salter said. 'Jake is your—lover?' He cleared his throat to speak more distinctly next time.

'I thought I had made that clear.' Nelson's eyes widened in mock surprise.

'And he's jealous of this Julia Costa?'

'He's jealous of *everybody*.'

'Possessive, like,' Salter said, feeling every moment more and more comfortable in Nelson's world. Apart from Nelson's taste in partners, it all sounded very familiar. He stood up. 'I'll come by this afternoon and get a confirmation from your room-mate.'

Nelson laughed. 'We have separate rooms,' he said. 'When his mother comes to town we are just regular buddies. Besides, he *snores*.'

Salter smiled. He opened the door, then paused.

'Relatives,' he asked. 'Did Drecker have any?'

'A wife. She's out of town. I phoned her

with the news and she's flying in this afternoon. Say, I thought you guys were the ones who were supposed to know all this?' Nelson added in a teasing voice.

'We'd check it all out, Mr Nelson, but it's quicker to ask you. Thanks for the coffee. I'll be back this afternoon.'

★　　★　　★

He drove back to the station-house and parked his car. It was nearly lunch-time, so he walked over to his squash club where he had arranged for a game with one of the other beginners. They lumbered about the court, oblivious of the world for forty minutes, and then had a sandwich and a beer together. He had been playing squash for five months, and though he was still no good at all, he pursued the game with childish pleasure. He and his partners knew almost nothing about each other (he told them he worked for the metropolitan government) but the exercise, the anonymity, and most of all, the pleasure he got from competing again, something he had not had for years, made these games the high points in his week.

He walked back to his office feeling lighter, especially in the head, and greeted his sergeant.

'How are you, Frank?' he asked.

'What's that?' Gatenby asked.

'I said, how are you?'

'Nothing wrong with me,' the sergeant said in a puzzled voice. They had already met once that day, and Salter was not one of nature's constant greeters.

'I want you to check the neighbours around that fire, Frank. Find out if anyone saw anything suspicous last night.'

'Right. I'll put the boys on it.'

'Have them check every building that overlooks the store.'

'All right. Anything else?'

'Not yet. There will be, though. I think this one will take a lot of checking around.'

'Your wife phoned, to remind you of your doctor's appointment. Anything the matter, Charlie?'

Salter looked up, startled. Sergeants do not call inspectors by their first names unless invited, and in taking the privilege on himself, Gatenby was pointing out that the time had come for Salter to acknowledge his sergeant, instead of keeping him at arm's length. Salter felt rebuked and very slightly touched.

'I don't know what's wrong, Frank,' he

said. 'Nothing, probably. Some test turned their litmus paper blue. I don't know.'

Gatenby nodded sympathetically, and Salter started to write a report for his superintendent. After half an hour it was time to go back to Washington Avenue and interview Nelson's room-mate. He told Gatenby that if Drecker's widow called, he would see her in the morning, and left.

* * *

This time he found Nelson in a very upset state. His friend, Jake Hauser, had come and gone while Salter had been away, but not before their quarrel had been renewed and intensified. Nelson was so agitated he could hardly talk. Another person was with him now, an attractive black-haired woman in her early thirties, dressed in jeans and a T-shirt that left her midriff bare.

'I'm Christine Nader,' she said, after Salter had identified himself. 'I live across the hall. I came over to complain about the noise last night, but poor Dennis was in such a state I stayed around.' She was kneeling beside Nelson's chair, holding his hand, her back half-turned to the policeman.

Nice neighbour. Salter tried to repress the

thought that she was wasted on Nelson. It was the kind of thing Drecker probably said. 'You heard the argument last night?'

'Oh yes, indeedy. Loud and clear,' she said over her shoulder.

'Do you want a full account of our quarrel?' Nelson shouted, close to tears.

'No, sir. If this lady can confirm that you were here until one o'clock, that's all I need to know.'

'I can guarantee it, Inspector,' she said.

'Good.' Salter still had not sat down, but he moved across the room to avoid looking directly into the top of her T-shirt. 'And where will I find Mr Hauser?'

'You won't. He's gone for good.' Nelson's voice was defiant.

'Has he? Why?'

'Because I told him to.'

'Nevertheless I'd like to talk to him. Where do you suggest I look?'

'I haven't any idea. His parents live in South Porcupine, but you won't find him there.'

The woman continued to soothe him, patting his hand gently.

'Where does he work?'

'At Queen's Park. He's an accountant for the Ontario Government.' Each statement

37

increased Nelson's distress.

'I'll try there. I'll come back tomorrow and go over that list of dealers.'

Nelson looked away, and the woman grimaced at Salter to go.

From a phone booth on Spadina Avenue he established quickly that Hauser had not been in to work that day and had not called in. No one knew where he was. The first suspect.

★ ★ ★

It was nearly three o'clock. He was not due at the hospital until three-thirty, so he filled in the time by attending to an item on Annie's list—the screen door. There was a hardware store on Bloor Street, not far from the burned building, and Salter drove the few blocks to it. He started to explain his errand, but the owner was shaking his head and pursing his lips before he had finished.

'No way,' he said. 'No way. No way. No-o-o way.'

Salter waited for the little performance to finish and the explanation to begin.

'They put those wheels on in the factory,' the man said, shaking his head steadily, so that Salter wanted to lean over and place his hand on the man's scalp to stop him. 'No way you can repair those suckers by yourself.'

'You mean I have to take the door to the factory?' Salter asked.

'That's right,' the man said with the loud, dogmatic confidence of someone who didn't know what he was talking about. 'What make is it?'

'I don't know. Is it on the door?'

'Should be, shouldn't it? What *you* have to do is find out who makes the door and see if they do repairs. Probably means a new door. How old is it?'

'Ten years.'

At this the man closed his eyes, turned sideways to Salter and started shaking his head again. 'They won't be in business now,' he said eventually. 'These factories disappear overnight.'

'In which case, I have to have the whole goddam unit replaced?'

The man shrugged and opened his eyes. 'Looks like it,' he said. 'Tough tittie. I could be wrong, of course,' he added, leaving the policeman back where he started.

'Thanks,' said Salter, and left the store with the sense that the screen door was going to be a classic.

At the hospital the specialist asked him questions for ten minutes; most of them seemed irrelevant, or suggested diseases that Salter had not even thought of. The doctor seemed indifferent to the answers, even when Salter could not answer at all, as with 'Are you urinating more or less frequently in the past year than usual?'

Salter then undressed and lay down and stared first at the wall, then at the ceiling. The doctor was soon done. 'You can get dressed now,' he said and disappeared. When the policeman was buttoned up he went into the outer office where the nurse was waiting to go home. His next appointment, she said, was on Thursday for the same time, with the X-ray department.

'What for?' Salter asked.

She replied in medical jargon which meant nothing to Salter.

'Did the doctor find anything, did he happen to tell you?' he asked.

'The doctor will send a full report to your family doctor,' the nurse said, adjusting her scarf in a mirror. 'Do we have his name?'

'I don't know. Do you?'

She put down her purse and went to a

filing cabinet where she found Salter's file. She looked at the single sheet of paper it contained. 'Dr Blostein?' she asked.

'That's right.'

She switched off the light and eased Salter into the corridor. 'We'll let him know,' she said.

★   ★   ★

At home Annie was waiting for news and Angus was in his room, waiting. He dealt with Angus first by knocking on his son's door, listening for a reply, and letting himself in when none came.

Angus was sitting in the exact centre of his bed, his knees up to his chin. Salter sat down.

'You got any more skin books in the house?' he asked.

Angus shook his head.

'Good. If you have, get rid of them tonight. They upset your mother. They don't upset me, I've seen them before. You want to talk?'

Angus shook his head again. He met Salter's eyes and looked back down at his feet. By now, Salter thought, he will have checked around at school and found out what usually happened to his pals when they got caught. What did happen? He pondered what

41

his own father would have done in the circumstances, but the question was absurd. In Salter's childhood, pornography consisted of sepia photographs that dated from the Twenties. The women in the pictures looked, to a fourteen-year-old, like aunts, and the men, mustachio'd with gleaming hair parted in the middle, like music-hall performers caught between changes. He had made no connection between the activities of these foreign-looking people and his own desires.

His father had said nothing of any kind on the subject. Talk of sex, like swearing, was forbidden in the house, and Salter carried into his teens the impression that his parents had banished that part of the world from their lives. One day, when Salter was sixteen, his father suddenly told him a very dirty joke as they were walking along the street, and Salter realised that his father was now treating him as a man, but he was too shocked to reply in kind.

Now he looked at his son and wondered how they would get through the next five years. Probably it would not be as long as that. In his own day most first-year undergraduates were still virgins, but nowadays they were all screwing in grade ten, weren't they?

Angus continued to observe his bare feet while Salter tried to find an exit line. There was a small pustule on the boy's neck, and a hint of hair on his lip, but underneath there was the innocent ten-year-old face of yesterday, and underneath *that* was the little boy he had taken to play in the sandpit in Oriole Park. Age, Salter thought, was something one's friends and relatives wore on top of the real person that you had known all along. The one or two acquaintances he still knew from his schooldays had not changed in thirty years—they had merely put on age as they had put on weight, a superficial change that looked like reality to the outsider, but to someone who had known them all along seemed no more than a kind of make-up.

He got up from the chair and patted the boy on the shoulder. 'See you later,' he said. Angus nodded, but did not look up, and Salter left.

Downstairs Annie was preparing some kind of curry. He poured himself a bottle of beer and walked out to the back porch, or 'deck' as it was known in his neighbourhood. Salter had married above himself—his wife came from an Establishment family in Prince Edward Island, and he met her and wooed her while he was recovering from the wreck of his first marriage. His own background was solidly lower-class. His father had been a maintenance man for the local streetcar company; his mother came from England at fourteen, shipped out by an orphanage to work as a domestic servant. Salter was wary of his wife's class, and of his own middle-class status, and he kept his distance from both by calling the garden the 'yard' and by eating his dinner at noon and his supper at night.

'What did you say to Angus?' Annie whispered in his ear.

'I told him to keep the skin books out of the house.'

'Is that all? Aren't you going to talk to him?'

'I don't know,' Salter said, who didn't. 'What about? They get it all in school, don't they?'

'It's not the same. He needs someone to put it all in some kind of context.'

'Shall I tell him how on our first night I put a rose between your legs because I'd read that someone did that in a book to show how beautiful he thought *IT* was? And you woke up in hysterics because you thought the rose was a spider?'

'Charlie, he needs someone to *talk* to him.'

'All right, all right. I'll do something. Leave it alone for now, will you?'

Angus came in the room behind them and sat down at the dining table. Annie called Seth and they began to eat. Annie gave a bright account of her day at work, a day in which she located an old gas station of the Forties, constructed to look like a sugar-candy house in a fairy story—a style widely used once but now nearly all gone. Seth had a story to tell about a temporary master at his school whom he described as a 'real lunch-box'. Angus said nothing and left the table as soon as he had finished.

Annie and Salter took their coffee out on to the back porch where the superb weather was just beginning to turn cool.

'Did you see the specialist?' she asked, when they were alone.

'Yes.'

'What did he say?'

'Nothing. His nurse said I have to go for some X-rays on Thursday.'

'What for?'

'Christ knows. I don't.' Back came the black wave that he had kept at bay for a few hours. He changed the topic. 'I got a new assignment today. Homicide.'

'Are you pleased?'

45

'It's better than organizing the leave rosters.' Salter waved away a wasp. 'This job of yours going to keep you busy?'

'I think so, for a little while.'

Salter grunted.

He was not yet quite used to a working wife. She had broken him in gently: in June she had announced that she was bored and they had talked about things she could do to get her out of the house; in July she had let him know that courses in French or getting into volunteer work was not what she had in mind. She wanted a job, a real job. She ran the house with her left hand, the boys were old enough not to set fire to it, and she needed, she said, a life, maybe even a career. A sign of the times, but at the bottom of his mind Salter feared letting her out of purdah in case she found out what alternatives the world had to offer to marriage to a police inspector whose career had come to a halt once and only now was showing signs of life again.

At first her job had been part-time, between ten and three, and Salter hardly noticed it and never inquired. When he thought about it he both believed and did not believe that she lived in a glamorous world filled with smooth bastards in Italian clothes.

46

He had never quite overcome the feeling of enormous luck at getting Annie in the first place (or rather, second place, after his brief, disastrous marriage to a flower-child who promptly took up arms against the Establishment, including Salter, so actively that the marriage shattered within a year). Salter was uxorious without being submissive, and while he had enough sense not to want to keep Annie in a doll's house, he feared for his safety whenever she spread her wings. He could not imagine life without her, but he sometimes thought that he might leave her so that he would no longer have to worry about her leaving him.

'It's not going to interfere with you. Aren't you glad for me?' she said.

'Oh, I am,' he lied. He waved another wasp away. 'Goddam wasps.'

'There's a nest. Outside the bathroom window.'

Salter looked up. A small brown globe about the size of a melon had appeared between the bathroom window and the screen.

'Knock it down,' he suggested.

'It isn't that easy. You might have to get a head net and some gloves.'

'*I* might leave it. They go to sleep in the

winter.'

'Then we'll have to get the screen door fixed. They are coming in the third floor.'

'I found out today that to fix the third floor we might have to take the back wall off the house.'

'Why don't you ask someone about it?'

'Who? What? I've tried,' Salter snapped in frustration. The phrase 'Why don't you...' was second only to 'By the way...' in making him angry. For all the progress that women had made, Annie, and most women in Salter's experience, responded to a difficult situation with a 'Why don't you'. Usually it involved a tricky or embarrassing situation, such as 'Why don't you ask the captain why the ship has stopped?' The classic 'why-don't-you' occurred when they were lost in a car on a trip to New York. Annie said, 'Why don't you ask that policeman if we are in Manhattan yet?' Salter did, and the cop said, 'Well, that's Central Park, bud, and I don't think they moved it lately.' But, as Annie said, she didn't see why women should have to ask all the potentially dumb questions.

'It has to be fixed, Charlie.'

Salter sighed. There was too much going on. 'I know. Right now, though, dear, just at this moment, fuck it, eh?'

He changed the subject. 'What do you know about antique dealers?' he asked. 'A store run by someone called Drecker out past Honest Ed's burned down last night. The owner died in the fire. Ever heard of it? It was called The Bottom Drawer.'

'A *real* antique shop?'

Salter shook his head. 'I doubt if your mother would bother with it,' he said. 'More of a—what-do-call-it—collectibles store. You know, junk. The lower end of the trade anyway. Antique apple-corers, but mostly second-hand stuff.'

'I knew some of the stores on Markham Street. Was it about that level? They are sort of off-Broadway.'

'Not even that, I think. Off-off-Broadway, if anything.'

'No. Never heard of it. But Jenny would know. Why don't you give her a call?'

Salter brightened. 'That's a thought. I'll ask her out to lunch.'

'She'll love that,' Annie said, slightly mocking.

Jenny Schumann was an antique dealer in Yorkville, an old friend who had employed Annie occasionally on a part-time basis before she had the children. She had been declaring

49

her interest in Salter, loudly and publicly, ever since she had met him, coupled with the assurance that only her friendship with Annie prohibited her from seducing him. Salter enjoyed the game, Annie was vicariously flattered by it, and Jenny had become the only friend they had in common who kept no secrets from either of them. She assumed that neither Salter nor Annie ever confided in her about the other, and freely passed on to both what the other had said. This ought to have inhibited secrets, but it worked in another way. Once they had come to know her, both Salter and Annie used her as a kind of marriage counsellor, telling her the things— mostly trivial but occasionally something fundamental—that they wanted her to pass on without having the face to do it directly. Annie, for example, once told Jenny that she wished she could have a room of her own, a workroom. This was before she got a job. Jenny immediately told Salter, who then realised that what he had heard for years as a faint and wistful desire was a real need that he should respond to seriously.

'Keep your hands above the table,' Annie said, kissing Salter on the head as she passed into the kitchen.

'Can I take my shoes off?' he called.

'Okay,' Annie shouted from the top of the stairs, 'But not hers, you hear?'

Salter blushed, and laughed.

CHAPTER TWO

Next morning, he began by reading the report of the officers who had checked Drecker's neighbours. Nothing. Nobody had seen or heard anything unusual. The last item on the report dealt with something else. One of the men doing the check had found a gallon can of camp fuel, still half full, among the weeds in the laneway that ran behind the store. Salter reached for the phone, dialled the Fire Marshal's number, and asked for Hayes, the investigator.

'Camp fuel,' Salter said, after identifying himself. 'We've found a can of camp fuel. That would work like gasoline, right?'

'Just as good. It's more volatile than regular leaded gas. It's called naphtha, or white gas.'

'Who would use it, apart from campers?'

'A lot of people. It's a good cleaning agent, so the owner might have had some.'

'So there's no point checking around trying

51

to trace the can and who it was sold to?'

'I wouldn't think so. But that's *your* job, isn't it?'

'Yeah, thanks.' Salter put the phone down. 'Send it off for fingerprints, Frank, and get it analysed,' he said. 'And remind me to put that officer's name in the report.' If you've robbed Peter, he thought, remembering his short-tempered response to the constable guarding the fire, you can pay back Paul.

Gatenby looked up. 'Is it very helpful?'

Salter thought about it. 'It means the fire was probably set by someone who threw the can in the weeds,' he said. 'That's the way it looked, but it's nice to have a piece of solid evidence. If it's covered in fingerprints, it will be even nicer. Anything else?'

'Drecker's widow called. She'll be in all day. I must say she didn't sound too upset.'

'I might as well go over now.' Salter hummed a little and looked at his watch. 'Frank, do you know how I might get a screen door fixed? A sliding one. The wheel has come off.' Salter had no idea why he was asking Gatenby, except that the Sergeant sometimes wore little glasses like Pinocchio's father which gave him the air of a clever old craftsman.

'Who put the door in?'

It was an obvious question. 'Fred Staver. We still have his number. I'll ask him. Thanks. Next question. What would you do if you caught your boy reading skin magazines?'

'I don't have a boy, do I?'

'I know. But what would you do if you *had* one?'

'I know what my old dad did when he caught me.'

'What?' This might be something.

'First of all he took me down to the basement and made me burn the pictures in the furnace. We had a woodburner in those days. Then he explained to me how looking at pictures like that would make my eyes weak and make me old before my time. Then he asked me how I would feel if my mum should see them. Then he told me if ever he caught me with anything like that again he would put me in the Working Boys' Home. He wouldn't have me in the house, he said. Then he hit me, once on each side of the head.'

'Did it work?'

'Oh yes. He was a bricklayer. My ears were ringing for days.'

'Did you hold it against him later?'

'No. It could have been worse. One of my

pals got caught and *his* father set the minister on to him. He had to go to the minister's house and tell him all he'd been up to in that way during the week. They used to get down on their knees together and pray for help to keep the boy pure. Oh no. My old dad and I had a good laugh about it later.'

'Did he ever try to teach you anything about sex?'

'When I started out with girls he said to me, "Remember, son. A standing prick has no conscience." I didn't understand that for years. Then, on my wedding day he said, "From now on, whenever you find yourself laying next to a woman, make sure she's your wife." He used to talk like that.'

It was news from another age. 'Thanks, Frank. Not much help now, though.'

'He also used to say, "If you don't know what to do, don't do anything." I've often found that useful.'

'I wish I could. But Annie's nagging me. She wants me to talk to him.'

'Take him fishing. You used to like that, and isn't that what they tell you to do. "Be a pal to your son."' There was no irony in Gatenby's voice.

Salter looked at him in surprise. 'I think you've got something,' he said after a few moments. He stood up and put on his jacket. 'Now I'm off to the bereaved widow. I'll call in at noon if anyone wants me.'

'If anyone inquires, I'll tell them you're busy. You are, aren't you?'

★　　★　　★

When Albany Avenue north of Bloor Street was first developed, families were bigger and automobiles fewer, so the houses were built with lots of rooms and jammed close together. Now that many of the houses have been carved into flats, the street is permanently full of cars, and the few narrow driveways all have signs warning against parking in front of them.

Drecker's home turned out to be a duplex badly in need of paint and repairs. The two balconies, one on each storey, looked unsafe, and the steps up to the front porch were starting to rot. Salter pressed the bell and heard someone coming downstairs. A large blonde woman opened the door. Behind her, a tiny hallway led immediately to the stairs to the upper apartment.

'Mrs Drecker?'

'Yes. You the policeman? Come on up.' She had a loud, metallic voice that banged on

55

Salter's eardrums.

He followed her up the stairs, along a bare, uncarpeted passage to a front room overlooking the street. The room was crammed with old furniture, including six ratty armchairs, much of it, Salter guessed, lodged there until it could be sold. A few dusty-looking pictures hung on the walls, and in the centre of the ceiling hung a huge bronze chandelier with a single light-bulb in one of its sockets.

'You want a soft drink? I don't have anything else,' she asked. She was in her mid-forties, dressed in a white linen tunic and sandals. Her yellow hair was braided around her head and her face was bare of make-up. The overall impression was of cleanliness: she looked sauna'd and scrubbed to the bone in contrast to the dilapidated paintwork and wallpaper of her home.

Salter declined the soft drink and produced his notebook. 'Mrs Drecker. You just got back to Toronto yesterday?'

'That's right. I was out west on holiday.'

They sat in facing armchairs. She folded her hands in her lap, looking no more disturbed than if she were responding to a public opinion pollster.

'Where, exactly?'

'Banff. The Solar Inn. It's a health camp. I go there every year.'

That accounted for the shining look. 'Mrs Drecker, we have to consider the possibility that your husband's death wasn't an accident. Did he have any serious enemies to your knowledge? Any quarrels, or feuds? Any business deals that might have brought him up against people who would do something like this?'

She brushed the suggestion aside with a gesture. 'He wasn't a fence, if that's what you mean, though he knew a couple. He didn't mind where the stuff came from (though he liked to *know*), as long as he could make a nice profit. But he didn't deal in the kind of thing that would be worth lifting—jewellery or silver. He stuck to furniture and he stayed inside the law, though he would swindle you if he could.' She spoke of her husband without malice, as an interesting character she had known.

'Had he "swindled" anyone lately that you know of?' he asked. There seemed no need to beat about the bush.

She shook her head. 'Not in a big way that I know of. When I say "swindled", I mean his idea of a good deal was to buy an old Ontario dresser from a bankrupt farmer for ten dollars and sell it for five hundred.'

And this was everyone's idea of Drecker. 'Doesn't everyone know about the value of stuff like that, nowadays?' he asked.

'You'd be surprised. There's still good pickings around here if you keep your eyes open.'

'And he did?'

'We both did. A lot of stuff these days comes out of garage sales. People moving house. We went round them together—I've got a good eye, myself, and most weekends we picked up a truckload. We usually found three or four things we could put through the shop, and the rest of it we'd get rid of at our own sales.'

'You *held* garage sales?'

'Sure. About once a month.'

'Where?'

'Different places. Lots of garage sales are phoney, didn't you know that? All you need is a place—a vacant lot will do—that you can rent for a few dollars. You can put up a lot of signs, and everyone comes looking for a bargain.'

Bunch of crooks, thought Salter, and made a mental note to tell Annie, who was fond of going round the neighbourhood sales on Saturday mornings. 'I gather you helped your husband run the store?' he asked.

She shook her head. 'We were partners, but I never went near the store when it was open. I have my own life.'

'Were you surprised at the news?'

'Sure I was surprised. Cyril was good at looking after number one. Besides, no one ever threatened him that I know of. As I said, he wasn't big league.'

Was she stone deaf, he wondered? Her voice seemed to be coming from an old gramophone, turned up to full volume. 'Why was he in the store that night? Did he often stay out all night?'

'I don't know, probably a woman. Look, Inspector, Cyril and I were partners. We got married ten years ago, but it didn't take, if you know what I mean. We didn't live together as man and wife after a few months. But, as I say, I've got a good eye, and I was useful to him. Besides, it was my money that set him up. So we became partners, legally. We still lived here but we left each other alone. We had separate rooms, and sometimes I cooked a meal—though I don't take much to that side of marriage, either— but mostly we went our separate ways. It worked out well for me. I play bridge, I practise yoga and go to health classes, and I have my own friends.'

All with soft, low voices, Salter hoped, unless they got together in a bomb shelter. 'You say, "some woman". Did your husband have many woman friends?' Other people's lives, or 'lifestyles', always sound weird if you think your own is normal.

'One at a time, usually. He never brought them here. That was our agreement. Separate lives. He used the room over the store, but I always knew who it was.'

'And who was it, lately?'

'Someone who worked in a furniture store at the other end of Bloor Street. Most of his women came through the trade.' Drecker's women might have been a hobby he had, like keeping exotic pets.

'You know her name?'

'It's above the phone in the kitchen. Hold on.' She disappeared into the back of the apartment and reappeared with a slip of paper in her hand. 'Julia Costa,' she said. 'You want her address?'

Salter took it down, checking it against the same address Nelson had given him. A small world. 'Will your husband's death change things very much for you, Mrs Drecker? You don't seem very upset.' What would the signs of grief be in Boadicea?

'Don't I?' She said nothing for a long time. Then: 'I told you, Inspector, Cyril and I were partners. I'm sorry he's dead, but I may be better off because of it. We insured each other and I'll own the business now, so in that way I'll be ahead of the game. On the other hand, it's been convenient for me sometimes as well as for him to be officially married to someone.' She let the remark hang in the air. 'I've been thinking. I'll have to reorganize myself. Yes, I'm sorry Cyril is dead, but I have no deep feelings about it.'

That seemed to be that. 'You'll be staying here for a while?'

'Yes. I own this building now, as well as the shop. I might sell it and move a little closer to my health club. I don't know. I'll be staying here for a few months, anyway.'

Salter stood up and put away his notebook. A thought seemed to strike him. 'What about your husband's assistant? How long has he been working in the store?' He tried to sound casual, ticking off the routine questions.

'Dennis? A year or so. Why?'

'He didn't seem to like your husband.'

'No. He didn't.'

Salter waited for some more.

'You've met him,' Mrs Drecker said. 'He's a pansy. Cy made fun of him, but Dennis

61

wouldn't hurt a fly.'

'What about his friend?'

'What about him?'

'Would he?'

'Because he's gay, you mean?' She was belligerent, challenging.

For Christ's sake, Salter thought. You started this. 'Whether he's straight, gay, or anything else,' he said.

'I don't know. I've never met him. I doubt it. If Dennis is harmless, his friend is, too, I would think.'

She's probably just defending alternative lifestyles, Salter guessed, having dropped out of the housewife role herself. He nodded to finish the interview, and started down the stairs. It was time for lunch with Jenny.

★　　★　　★

'Miss Schumann is expecting you. She said she'd be right down,' the assistant said. A nice young girl with a pear-shaped figure and her hair in a bun, an old-fashioned type who reminded Salter of the trainee librarians of his youth. Salter thanked her and walked round the store.

Jenny Schumann specialized in antique silver. Her shop took up the ground floor of a converted house; above it was a shop that sold old maps; the third floor Jenny had converted into an apartment for her own use. She had bought the house for thirty thousand dollars in the Fifties and remodelled it herself. It was now worth three-quarters of a million. Her store was like the chapel of a radical modern religion where the artifacts of an older faith were on display. The rug was rich and dark; the white walls were pierced by several small windows, each of which was lit from within to make a showcase to display a teapot (Georgian, $10,000) or a silver and lead glass desk set (about 1860, English, slight chip, $1,500). On one wall, a row of locked glass cases held a lot of small objects, snuff-boxes and such. The other merchandise was set out on appropriate altars. A coffee service with sharp edges was centred on a long, black, highly-polished table, also for sale. Two objects that were either vases or giants' mead cups were displayed on what looked, to Salter's surprise, like a battered card-table, but turned out to be a 'coaching table' (probably early 19c). In all, about a dozen pieces of expensive furniture displayed a large fortune in silver objects, mostly designed for eating and drinking.

While he waited for Jenny, Salter amused

himself by pricing the merchandise, playing the game he usually played in these circumstances, called 'Do I have any taste, of any kind whatsoever?' Because of the one on display in the window, he concentrated on teapots, of which there were three for sale. After looking at all three several times in turn, he had no trouble rejecting a Victorian horror, valuable because of its weight, no doubt, but with none of the quiet classical good lines of the other two, Salter told himself. But he could not decide between these two, one of which was square in design, and the other bulbous.

'Which one do you like?' asked Jenny, who had appeared beside him.

Salter decided not to play. 'That one,' he said, pointing to the Victorian monstrosity, and began preparing his defence, the view of the common man who likes a bit of decoration on his teapot.

'You have exquisite taste, Charlie. That's the best thing in the store.'

You can't win, he thought, but he accepted the compliment as his by right. He gave her a hug, and helped her on with her coat. He had booked a table at the café in Hazelton Lanes, and they arrived early enough to be given a place in the corner. As usual, she made it the focus of the restaurant. Pairs of women had watched them come in and then turned to each other to wonder what the connection would be between them. It was not her beauty, although it was from her that Salter had discovered how attractive a woman of fifty could be. She was carefully made up (Annie had explained to him once how it was done), and the effect, as he said to Annie, was like a softly-lit painting, which made Annie laugh out loud. Dark hair worn long, with enough grey in it to admit her age; she was tall and thin, and she liked velvet. Today the colour was black, with a lot of gold jewellery. Dark grey stockings with, Salter noted, very pretty black and gold shoes. He had a thing about shoes.

She was rich, of course, but other people are rich without having her aura, like, he thought, like—like—a queen who has been elected. Content with his simile, and aware of the eyes of the world, he bent over and kissed her. She smoked too much, and her breath smelled faintly of seaweed, but Salter didn't mind that either.

'My knight in shining sackcloth,' she declared in a charred voice that reminded him by contrast of Mrs Drecker.

'What do you mean?' he asked, surprised.

65

He was wearing his normal outfit of grey flannel trousers, dark blue tweed jacket, white shirt and blue tie with red geese. 'Something wrong?' he asked, looking down at himself.

'Wrong? What could be wrong?' she said. 'The same clothes you've had on for fifteen years to my knowledge. How could they be wrong?'

'I bought this coat last year in Eaton's. It was on sale,' Salter protested, and then the penny dropped. 'You've been talking to Annie,' he said. 'Well, these are my plain clothes, see. They are the ones that make me inconspicuous so no one can tell I'm a cop, see.'

She made a charade of nearly falling off her chair laughing. 'Are you kidding? Half the people in this café think you are about to arrest me.'

Salter looked around and a number of heads clicked back into place.

'What do you want me to wear?' he asked. 'A gold windbreaker? Earrings? You want me to get my hair done in ringlets? I'm a square, for God's sake.'

'No, Charlie, no. Just a coat that fits you. And a decent haircut. And even squares don't use the term any more.'

'I just got this haircut. It cost me ten bucks.'

'On sale?' She sat grinning at his wounded pride. 'Tell Annie I tried,' she said. 'Anyway, who cares. If Annie doesn't want you, I'll take you, Eaton's basement wardrobe and all. It's just your body I'm interested in. Superman in his Clark Kent rig, that's you.'

Salter looked smug. The polite greetings had been exchanged; the conversation could now proceed.

'Tell me about antique dealers,' he asked. 'I'm investigating a death by fire of an antique dealer and I'd like to get filled in on how he operated.'

'Cyril Drecker?'

He nodded.

'Not really in my world, although I knew him slightly. He wasn't an antique dealer. He was a second-hand dealer. There's a difference. Let's order first.' There was no Anglo-Saxon business with Jenny of trying to catch the waiter's eye with a genteel wave of the menu. 'Waiter,' she called in a Tallulah Bankhead summons, and he came, smiling, immediately.

She ordered fish and a glass of white wine. Salter ordered a veal and partridge pie, at her insistence, and beer. When the drinks came, he swallowed half his beer at a gulp as she watched admiringly.

'So greedy,' she said, making it sound like a sexual attribute.

He wiped his mouth with the back of his hand so as to be in character, and started again. 'You knew Drecker,' he prompted.

'Very slightly. I bought a Victorian hip-flask from him once. A touch of sleaze about him, I thought. I made sure I got full provenance.'

'Why would he sell it to you?'

'Because it was too good for him to handle. I imagine he did that with a lot of stuff.'

'You mean that he would pick up something dirt cheap, sell it to you for three times what he paid, and you sell it for twice as much again?' he asked, teasing her about the fat profits she made.

She threw the tease back. 'That's right. My father used to say, "You buy something for a dollar, sell it for two and make one per cent profit." He thought people who made twenty per cent profit were greedy.' She made a face at him.

'Did Drecker have a reputation, a bad one, in the trade?'

She shrugged. 'He might have. I don't hear much talk. The dealers I know don't sit around in some antiquaries' handout, swapping theives' gossip, Charlie. If I have any doubts, I just don't buy. If there are any fences in the trade, I don't know them. Try your pawn squad.'

'What about your own professional association? Would they know?'

'I doubt if he was a member of the Canadian Antique Dealers' Association, Charlie. We're a choosy lot. Besides, I told you, Drecker was a second-hand dealer, not an antique dealer.'

'What's the difference?'

'Antiques are at least a hundred years old—that's the difference. And we don't need a licence to operate.'

'Second-hand dealers do.'

'Sure. And they have to register everything that comes off the street with you, the police, and they can't sell it for fifteen clear days. Ask the pawn squad.'

'I will. I should have already. But what about the guy himself? Did you get any kind of impression? As a man, I mean.'

'What do you mean?'

'I think he was a bit of a womaniser,' Salter said.

'Was he? I can't help you on that one, either. You know me—I'm only interested in short-haired policemen. Are you looking for a love-triangle?'

Salter shook his head. 'I don't know what I'm looking for.'

The food arrived and Salter got on with his pie while Jenny stabbed at bits of her fish.

'Interrogation over, Charlie? Can you put the lunch on expenses now?' she asked after a few minutes.

'I'll pay for it myself, with cash, so that Annie won't see the charge slip and find out about us.' He leered at her, beginning the game again, and pushed his empty plate to one side. Jenny nodded to the hovering waiter, who slid into gear immediately to bring them their coffee.

'Would that we could.' She sighed theatrically. 'Which reminds me about Annie. I saw a Bristol glass decanter to match the two she already has. It's perfect—original stopper and everything. The gold is a bit faded but the label is clear—"Hollands". She has "Brandy" and "Rum", doesn't she?'

'Yes. Where did you see it?'

'I'll give you the address. It's in Hamilton.'

'Hamilton? I thought all the real antique dealers were around *this* area. Hamilton's all steelmills, isn't it?'

'Nice of you to say so, Charlie, but it isn't

70

true. Two of the best dealers in the province are in Streetsville and St Catherines. The dealer in Hamilton wants three hundred, and he'll keep it until you can get down there.'

'Done.' What a stroke of luck, he thought. Christmas for Salter was infected, poisoned, every year by his inability to find the perfect present for Annie. He had no confidence in his own taste, but he felt a compulsion to surprise her on Christmas morning with exactly the right toy. He had tried spending a lot of money, but that hadn't worked. She took the matched set of cow-hide luggage back to Simpson's and bought a washing machine instead. The clothes he bought didn't fit, and the jewellery was ugly (although he had once bought her a ring she liked, so he bought her a ring every year for the next five years until she asked him to stop).

Solving the problem with a certain winner this early in the year would mean he could look forward to Christmas like everyone else. All he had to do now was find the right book, the ideal record, and a big bottle of bath oil of a kind that she had never used before. A week's work, but a piece of cake now that the chief problem was solved.

'I said "how's everything at home"?' Jenny

71

asked, kicking his ankle. 'Wake up, lover.'

'Sorry. Fine. No. It's not so good.' And he told her about Angus. 'Annie thinks I should talk to him,' he said. 'But I don't know what the hell there is to say. So he's looking at dirty books. So what? It doesn't mean he's a sex maniac.'

'Is that what Annie said?'

'Not exactly.'

'What did she say exactly?'

'She said she wants me to help him put it into a context. That's the word she used.'

'What did you say?'

'I cut her off. I said I'd think about it.'

'Charlie, maybe she doesn't mean it that simplistically. Annie isn't silly. She knows how things have changed.'

'What are you talking about?'

'You're a policeman, Charlie. Gorgeous, but a policeman. Maybe just a little bit conservative. Couldn't Annie be saying the opposite of what you think?'

'I still don't know what you are talking about.'

'Look. If I caught—oh Christ, "caught"—if I found any skin books in one of my kids' cupboards, I'd leave them there. They're his, aren't they? But I would ask him what he got out of them. Then I have a feeling we'd all look at them together, if it didn't bother him.'

'You'd *what?*'

'I'd look at them with him. Then maybe we could get something going about pornography, sex, love—the whole bit.'

'But Angus is fourteen! Anyway, you don't have any kids.'

'If I did, I wouldn't go hairy over a couple of skin magazines.'

'I'm not. Annie is.'

'Oh, for God's sake, don't be so damned dense. Sorry. Look, Charlie, it sounds to me as if Angus is as frightened of you as you were of your father. Frightened to tell you what is happening to him. Your house is full of taboos, and what Annie wants you to do is not intimidate Angus any more. Talk to him. Talk to him like a human being.' Jenny sipped her coffee, slightly agitated.

Salter was very disturbed. Here was all the trendy psycho-jargon that was the staple of the Saturday newspaper columnists, in articles that Salter regularly jeered at, coming to him now from someone real, over the age of twenty-nine. Could it be true?

'You mean Annie and Angus, and maybe even Seth, are waiting for me to relax and talk about sex?'

'It sounds like it to me.'

'Maybe they talk now, behind my back?'

'Maybe.'

'Then why hasn't Annie said anything, done anything?' Salter asked, trying to find an alternative villain.

'She probably has, but you always cut her off. I don't know, I'm not there.'

'You make me feel like a bloody Victorian.'

'I think the boys see the policeman in you more than the father.'

'Thank you, Ann Landers.'

'Look at you now. Let's talk about something else. Who have you arrested lately?'

But Salter was too disturbed to give much attention to any other topic. After a few minutes, Jenny got up to go. She looked around the restaurant, then kissed him on the cheek. 'Whatever else you do, Charlie, tell Angus you love him. If you do, that is. Say, "I love you, Angus." See what happens. It's the big thing in pop psychology. That, and touching.'

'I can't do that,' Salter said.

'Why not?'

'I'm a Canadian,' he said.

She laughed and patted his cheek.

Salter sat at the table for a few more

minutes feeling too much alone in a changing world. Then he walked through Yorkville to his car and sat in the parking lot for a few minutes. But the mood hadn't passed when he drove off to meet Nelson in his apartment.

★　　★　　★

'Here you are,' Nelson said. 'Everybody he's dealt with in the last three months. All the ones who demanded receipts, that is.' Nelson had made a neat list. He had calmed down from his distress of the day before, but he looked at if he had not slept.

Salter took the list and glanced at it. 'Any word from your friend?' he asked casually.

'No. Have you?'

'Not yet. He hasn't shown up for work yet. Tell me who these people are. How did Drecker come to deal with them?'

'They are all specialty dealers,' Nelson said. 'This one, for instance, is an interior decorator on Davenport Road. He buys any garden ornaments we get.'

'What was this for?' Salter pointed to an item of two thousand dollars sold to a dealer in Yorkville.

'I'm not sure. He's Toronto's biggest dealer in Japanese prints, and I never saw anything around our store he would be interested in. You'll have to ask him yourself. Drecker might have got something from an old Japanese gentleman who's been coming in lately. He bought a wooden box from us three weeks ago, and he's been back twice while I've been in the shop. Drecker used to deal with him upstairs—he always did his important deals up there—and he never told me anything about him and I never asked. But after the last time, Drecker told me to say he was out if the Japanese ever came back. Maybe the guy wanted his money back, something Drecker never did.'

'If Drecker was involved in anything crooked, really crooked, would you know about it?'

'Probably not. He liked me to think he was always wheeling and dealing, but I think that was mostly BS. He would never take any risks. He was too wary not to cover himself six ways at once, even when he was cheating on his income tax. Still, as I say, if he was on to anything big he wouldn't brag about it to me. But I doubt if Drecker was mixed up with the mob.'

'Is the mob into antiques, Mr Nelson?'

'I thought they were into everything.'

'You've been watching too much American

television. There's a five-year lag between the US and Canada, in crime as well as culture. It gives us a chance to know what to expect. We watch television, too, to see what ideas our local villains might be picking up. Do you do any dealing on your own?' Salter asked suddenly.

'Sometimes. I pick up things at auctions, and Drecker used to let me sell them through the store, for a percentage of the profit. Nothing very much, but I *am* trying to learn the business, and Drecker didn't pay much. He said I ought to pay *him*, as if I was indentured or something.' Nelson stared at Salter, inviting him to share his astonishment.

'Why did you stay there? You didn't like him much, did you?'

'I loathed him, I told you. But look in the papers. There aren't many advertisements for "Antique Dealer's Assistant Wanted". I was learning something, and getting to know a few of the other dealers. As soon as anything better cropped up I would have moved. In the meantime I had to eat, and if things got too rough I could always go back to my old trade.'

'Which is?'

'I was a librarian at Douglas College. I left

because I couldn't stand the politics.'

'Politics? In a college library?'

'Really. You have no idea.'

'Well, well. Thank God we don't have any of that in the Force.'

Salter put the list back in his pocket. 'I'll have a word with some of these people. Apart from this lot, you know of no other enemies Drecker had? He hadn't gotten into any arguments lately?'

'The man I told you about, the one who remodelled the bathroom.'

'Darling?'

Nelson nodded. 'And me. But you've checked up on me, I suppose.'

'Not yet. Do you ever go camping, Mr Nelson?'

Nelson grinned. 'You mean locally, or the great outdoors?'

'I mean back-packing, Mr Nelson.' It was not a serious inquiry, for Salter found it hard to visualize Nelson waking beside Lake Onatonga, greeting the dawn with a cheer.

'Ah ha!' he said. 'You've found a clue. Someone left a tin of Eddie Bauer's waterproof matches at the scene of the crime.'

'You *do* go camping, then?'

'I did once, Inspector. Once and once only.

Jake was keen on canoeing when I met him, and he persuaded me to go on a trip with him this spring into Algonquin Park. What a weekend! To start with, Jake insisted on being very authentic. No artificial firelighters, all dried food—have you ever lived on dried foods for three days? When we came out I had to have four jelly doughnuts immediately. Jake didn't think we should take anything to drink, either—no wine, no gin, nothing. We had a row about that. Can you imagine the voyageurs as teetotallers? I finally insisted on a mickey of scotch for medicinal purposes. I figured one large, very large, drink at night, just for me while Jake drank his bark tea or whatever. Of course, when I opened it the first night he offered to keep me company—without approving of it, mind you—so there wasn't enough to last the trip. The whole expedition was like that. First there were the mosquitoes. At every portage we had to drape ourselves in nets and carry the canoe through thick clouds of them. At night we huddled in this little survival tent, listening to them on the outside, trying to get at us. I was covered in bumps and itching like the owner of a flea circus.' Nelson was getting more and more animated. 'And filthy! My God, does anyone realize how dirty the great outdoors is? What with mosquito repellent, the smoke from the cooking fires, and the grease—everything that isn't dried is fried, Inspector—I've never felt so squalid. And Jake was unbearable. He had bought a lot of equipment—Swiss army knives and gadgets for smoking fish and the like—which he wanted to try out. It nearly finished us, I can tell you. I took a week to get back to normal and we agreed that he and I would never share the outdoors again. Yes, I've tried camping.'

And you've told this story a few times at parties. 'And your friend Hauser is an experienced camper now, I take it?'

'I suppose so.' Nelson quietened down and began to stammer slightly as he realized the message he had conveyed to Salter. 'Why? Did you find a clue? Lots of people go camping, you know.'

'I know. I'm asking them all.' Salter put away his notebook.

'Have you checked up on my alibi yet?'

'Not yet.' And there isn't much need if you are so keen on it, Salter thought. Was he trying to change the subject? 'I still have to see this Julia Costa. I'll do that this afternoon or tomorrow. Have you spoken to her yet?'

'Oh, sure. But I really was with her. She

was wonderful.'

That word again. To Salter's generation a 'wonderful person' meant Mahatma Gandhi or Schweitzer in Africa. You expected to meet maybe two in a lifetime. Now it just meant 'nice' and he wished teachers in grade school would warn students against it, as he had been forbidden to use 'nice' by his seventh-grade teacher. Salter tried for an unsettling remark. 'Anyway,' he said, smiling, 'as Drecker's girlfriend she would hardly cover for his killer, would she?'

'You know about that, do you? Well, I don't care. She's a wonderful person.'

'That's nice,' Salter said, and left.

He looked over the list before he drove off. Most of them could be left to Gatenby, but he decided to call on the Japanese specialist himself to find out what was worth two thousand dollars, and that put the interior decorator on Davenport on his route back to the office. He drove north on Spadina across Bloor and became involved in the tangle of one-way streets that is designed to protect the area from people who wish to drive through it, streets that change direction at every intersection, so that navigating them is like tacking against a high wind. Eventually he fought his way through to Avenue Road and turned into Cumberland Street, where he made a slightly illegal turn into the municipal parking lot.

He found MacLeod's gallery tucked away in an alley. There was none of the hurly-burly of commerce here. This was a gallery with a dozen oriental-looking pictures hung on the walls with small price labels beneath them. Salter spent his usual few minutes looking at the pictures, trying to see what made the difference in desirability between those priced at fifty dollars and one on sale for three thousand. He decided he liked the three-thousand-dollar picture best, but only just; say, twenty dollars' worth more.

In the middle of the gallery, behind a desk, a bushy-haired man was reading invoices. He looked too young to be the owner of what was obviously a very successful business (the gallery had half-a-dozen people in it), but he was sorting paper with authority.

'Mr MacLeod?'

'Inspector?'

'Am I that obvious?'

'I've been expecting you.'

'Have you now,' Salter said, and waited.

'Why don't you sit down?' MacLeod said, gesturing to a chair beside him. 'We can talk here, if you like, Hajime will look after the customers.' He pointed to a young Japanese who was laying out pictures on a large bench at the back of the gallery.

It was not the place Salter would have chosen, but MacLeod seemed to have a quiet voice, so no one would take any interest in their conversation.

'You know what I've come for?'

'Drecker. I read about it in the paper. I only dealt with him once but it was a big deal for him and I expect you found it in his books. Right?'

Salter nodded.

'He offered me a collection of Japanese prints and I bought some of them. I sold the lot in one go in a way I thought was odd, but now, Inspector, has turned out to be even odder.'

'A good deal for you?'

'I didn't even display them. But the man who bought them has disappeared, hasn't he?'

'You tell me, Mr MacLeod.'

'Ah! You don't know about him? Well, I'll tell you. His name is Gene Tanabe—I've sold stuff to him for years, ever since I opened. He's a dealer himself, but one of those who hates selling anything he really likes so he's got a pretty good private collection. I called him when this lot came in from Drecker and he flew in from Vancouver the next day and bought them all. He wanted to know where I got them so that he could get the others, and I gave him Drecker's address. He was very excited.'

'Do you know why? Collector's mania?'

'No.' MacLeod savoured what he was about to say. 'He said he knew the man who once owned them.'

'Did he?' Salter said, digesting this bit. 'Did he, indeed?'

'I asked him how Drecker had got hold of them and he said that was what he wanted to know, too. I asked him if the prints had been stolen and he said, perhaps, but he didn't think so. That was the last I saw of him. When I heard about Drecker, I called Gene's store in Vancouver, but they told me he was in Toronto, had been here a week. I thought that was a bit strange because he always calls on me. We are sort of friends now.'

'Could you describe him, Mr MacLeod?'

'About seventy-five, conservatively dressed, umbrella—the whole old Japanese gentleman bit.'

'Accent?'

'Oh no. He's a Canadian. He was born here, I'm sure—a nisei, at least.'

84

Salter formulated a question that was puzzling him.

'Prints, Mr MacLeod. I know they number prints nowadays when they run off a limited edition, but I thought that was a recent practice. Were these prints numbered? If not, how did Tanabe recognize them?'

'Do you know anything about Japanese art, Inspector?'

Salter shook his head. Or Canadian, or any other kind.

MacLeod opened a thick volume like a catalogue of wallpaper samples. Each page was a plastic envelope containing a picture. 'Let me give you a short course,' he said. 'Here we have a print by one of the best-known of the Ukiyo-e artists, Kuniyoshi, printed about 1840. It's a print of characters in a Kabuki drama. Now, look here. These marks were not on the original print, they are seals put on by collectors who owned the picture.' He pointed to some oriental-looking signs on the corner of the print.

'You mean you guys stamp every print?'

MacLeod's eyes glazed. 'No, no,' he said. 'These marks were only added by Japanese collectors of the past—the practice is frowned on now—not by every Tom, Dick and Harry over here. Let me get on. We can generally identify a print by its markings, then, but look at this, too.' He turned to a block of photographs. 'Here are six impressions of the same picture. You see how they differ? The results vary so much in light and shade that they are virtually all different pictures, and we can identify them as such.' MacLeod started to leaf through the book. 'Let me find two I can show you by way of comparison,' he said.

Salter said, 'There's an interesting one.' It was a picture of a couple enjoying each other in a position Angus would have recognized from the magazines he had been studying. Behind the couple, two ladies were seated on the floor. They seemed to be either applauding or praying. 'Nothing new under the sun,' Salter said. 'How much is that?'

MacLeod seemed surprised. 'You want to buy it?' he asked. 'Seven hundred and fifty.' He looked at Salter curiously.

'No, no, just joking,' Salter said, realizing what MacLeod must be wondering.

MacLeod closed the book and waited for Salter's next question.

'So Drecker sold you some prints, Tanabe came to town and bought them off you, claiming he recognized them, and disappeared. Right? How many prints were there altogether, and why didn't you buy them all?'

'They were a mixed lot. None of them was very valuable, but the ones I bought were by far the best—a Hiroshige, a couple of Shunko hosoban—'

'Could you write those down for me?' Salter interrupted.

MacLeod scribbled on a piece of paper. 'And three others,' he continued. 'You want their names?'

Salter nodded. 'What about the ones you didn't buy?'

'There were about ten more, but they were all in pretty poor condition.'

'Where would Drecker have got rid of them?'

'He *might* have sent them to an auction house. And a lot of antique stores carry a few Japanese prints.'

Salter thought about his next question. 'Was there anything to connect these prints? With each other, I mean.'

'You are asking me to speculate about them? About whether they were a collection?'

'Yes,' Salter said. 'That's what I would like you to do. Speculate about them for me.'

'They all had the same collector's seals on the back,' MacLeod offered.

'What does that mean?'

'It means they all passed through the same collector's hands. But not necessarily at the same time.'

'Nothing else struck you about them, as a group?'

'Like what?'

Salter shook his head. 'I don't know, Mr MacLeod.' He did, though. A bit of Sherlock Holmes stuff from MacLeod, like: 'These prints must have been assembled in a suburb of Yokohama in 1913, by a woman who had served at court...'

MacLeod waited patiently.

'Did he offer you anything other than prints?' Salter searched his mind for the word 'netsuke' but was unsure how to pronounce it.

'No.'

Now Salter had run out of questions. He stood up. 'That was the only time you saw Tanabe, then? And you have no Toronto address for him?'

'That's right and he hasn't been home for a week.'

'If he appears, would you let me know right away? You can tell him I'm looking for him,' he added, to get MacLeod off the hook of being disloyal to his friend.

'I don't think Gene could have anything to do with Drecker's store burning down. I'd vouch for him.'

'All I'm trying to do is find out what Drecker was up to lately, and with whom. Anyone who has dealt with him, like you, might be able to give me a lead.'

Now, Salter thought, as he walked to his car, I have another one who might have a grudge against Drecker: Gene Tanabe.

He made one more call, on the interior decorator. This one specialized, as he said, in 'tarting up old town houses', and he often included the garden in his design. Drecker routinely sold him any stone or concrete ornaments that he picked up.

Salter thanked him and checked his watch. He had begun a second, expensive half-hour in the parking lot, so he decided to treat himself to a bowl of goulash soup in the Coffee Mill, for Salter's taste, the best food in the area. While he ate, he listened to four America tourists taking the weekend off from being mugged in Detroit, enthusing about how clean Toronto was. Toronto the Clean, he thought. It's not much, but an improvement on Toronto the Good.

★ ★ ★

'Frank,' he said, back at the office, 'call the Vancouver cops and ask them if they know of a Gene Tanabe, pronounced "Tarnarbay". Here's his address. And call the pawn squad and see if anything is known about Drecker. And I want you to check up on this list of dealers—all of them did business with Drecker in the last three months. Leave those two, I've just seen those, but find out if any of the others had any unfinished business with Drecker. Do it yourself. Take the day tomorrow and work out a little story about having to wind up Drecker's legal affairs or some such horseshit, and watch for any funny reactions, all right?'

'I'll enjoy that, Charlie. I'll tell them I've got 'em on a list. I'll tell them I found the list in Drecker's safe-deposit box with crosses against some of the names.'

Salter laughed. 'Don't fuck around too much, Frank. You don't look the part for the heavy brigade. Just see if you can smell anything.'

'Right you are. Can I have a car?'

'Okay.' Salter made out a requisition.

Gatenby grinned with glee. 'Just like the TV. "Gatenby here, Homicide." This is great. I haven't been outside for months on a job. Should I pack a rod?'

The pawn squad called back in five minutes with the information that Drecker was licensed, that nothing was known about him, and that he had registered the box containing assorted knick-knacks aand pictures, value (estimated) $200, six weeks before, offered to him by a casual vendor.

Well, well, Salter thought. Does that put Drecker in the clear in whatever was going on? Not necessarily. Nelson had emphasized that Drecker was a careful man, careful enough to cover himself if something went wrong.

*   *   *

He spent the rest of the afternoon writing up his report, but before he went home he called on a colleague in the Homicide department, a man who had offered him a hand on his last case. Harry Wycke seemed pleased to see him and put to one side the paper he was working on.

'What's it these days, Charlie?' he asked. 'Another Montreal murder? You'll be doing us out of business.'

His tone was friendly, and it crossed Salter's mind that he had meant to invite

91

Wycke and his wife to the house after their last chat but he had put it off too long, until the detective would have been surprised by it. He told Wycke first of the case he was on, then, self-mockingly, of the trouble he was having with the screeen door, and finally about Angus. This last problem made him feel that he was lacking something, that if he were a proper father he would know what to do without going around asking people.

Wycke reassured him immediately. 'I don't know, Charlie. Raising kids, relating to them or whatever the bullshit term is nowadays, is bloody hard. Every Christly magazine has got an article on it, all different, but if you look around, it's gotta be mostly luck. I've got girls, so Shirley worries about all that. I'm the father figure; I just have to be careful they don't catch penis envy off me. But with boys I think the big risk would be trying to avoid all the wrong things that were done to you, you know what I mean? But how can you tell? I mean, look at Wilcott's kids. He did nothing for them—nothing. I don't think he even likes them. Straight A students, both of them, one's going to be a doctor and the other one's studying architecture. Then there's Joe Loomis's kids. You remember how Joe used to bore the ass off us in the canteen about how he was raising them? No, you wouldn't. You never ate there. Well, Joe started with Spock and bought a new book every year. Taught them all about liking themselves, stuff like that. So what happens? Poor old Joe is pinning all his hopes on the youngest one now—the other two have gone off to find themselves. They didn't finish school, can't hold a job—nothing. It's all in a play we did at school about a salesman who committed suicide. Nothing's changed. I don't think it matters a fuck what you do.'

'I need to try, Harry. Gatenby said I should take him fishing.' Salter watched Wycke for any trace of a smile.

'You like fishing? I never thought of you in the great outdoors, Charlie. A real townie, I figured.'

'I am. I don't spend my leaves canoeing the great Nottawasaga, but I like fishing and I never get to go. Got any suggestions? For a place, I mean. I think I'll go for a weekend.'

Wycke leaned back in his chair. 'I've got a place,' he said. 'You know that.'

'I didn't know that, Harry,' Salter said, embarrassed. 'I didn't come here on the scrounge.'

'Well, I have. You can have it if you want.'

Wycke's voice was neutral, uneager.

A silence had opened between them, but once raised, the subject had to be discussed.

'What kind of place is it? Do you ever rent it out?'

'No, I plead with people to use it, *if* they know what they are doing. I built the place myself, and it's not a cottage, it's a cabin. It's mosquito-proof, waterproof, and it has a Coleman stove for cooking, two Coleman lamps, and four bunks. No power, no water, just a shelter. But I'm careful who I let have it. You'd be surprised how many people think it sounds romantic, but when they get up there they are afraid to use the outhouse in case there's a bear hiding down below.'

Salter laughed. 'I'm not worried about bears snapping at my ass,' he said.

'So you can have it. But look, Charlie, don't come back and tell me you couldn't find the hot-water tap, will you? You get your water out of the river in a bucket. There are mice, spiders, big hairy bugs with two hundred legs, and at night it gets as cold as a witch's tit because it isn't insulated. There's a wood stove, but at this time of the year you'll wake up at four in the morning and see your breath. It doesn't have the woman's touch because my family don't like it. I do, though.'

Salter said, 'I worked at a fishing camp once on the English River near Kenora. We lived in cabins like that from April to October. I know how they work. Can I have it? I'll be able to show Angus how resourceful his old man is. Make up for not taking him to baseball and football games.'

'When? When do you want it?'

'The weekend after next if I can?'

'It's yours. Here.' Wycke opened a drawer. 'Map; list of instructions; I'll call the marina so they will let you have the boat; a picture of the cabin so you'll recognize it; and the key. There's one good rod up there, but you'll need to take up another one for the boy.'

'I appreciate it, Harry. Nice of you to let me have it.'

'No, it isn't. The more people use it, the less chance it will become derelict. People get to know when a cabin isn't being used and start nosing around. Enjoy yourself and bring back a list of stuff that's missing or needs repairing.' He consulted a piece of paper. 'According to the last guy, you'll need naphtha, salt and toilet paper. There's a store at the marina.' He looked at Salter. 'Maybe if you like it we could go up together some time.'

'All right. Let's talk about it when I get back.'

Salter left, wondering if he would have been as generous in the same position.

On the way home, he made another attempt to get a wheel for the screen door at a hardware store on Yonge Street run by three New Zealanders. Usually resourceful, they were unable to help.

'All I can tell you is that you aren't alone,' the owner said. 'The last guy who broke his screen door decided to sell his house rather than try to get it fixed.' They all roared with laughter.

*　　*　　*

'I thought you might like to go fishing with me one weekend,' Salter said after supper.

Angus looked as startled as if Salter had proposed skydiving together. 'With you?' he asked. 'We've never been before. I don't know how.'

'I do. Want to give it a try?'

Annie was looking at Angus so eagerly that he flinched. 'All right,' he said. 'When?'

'Next week. We'll go up Friday night and come back late on Sunday. This place is north of Parry Sound but we should get almost two days there.'

'What do I have to get ready?'

'I'll look after it all. There is some tackle up there and I can pick up the rest. We'll need some food.'

'I'll make chili and freeze it, and some hamburger patties—I'll freeze them, too, then all you have to do is cook them as they defrost. What do you want for breakfasts?' Annie asked.

Salter looked at her and she shut up, but she continued to look pleased.

★   ★   ★

When the dishes were done, Salter got out his notebook. 'What's a nisei?' he asked.

'A second-generation Japanese Canadian. Why?'

Salter told her.

'I know the gallery,' she said. 'He has some wonderful things. Now you tell me one. Where can I get some gnomes?'

'What?'

'Gnomes. You know, those plaster gnomes people used to have in their gardens. They are "in" again and I have to dress up a fashionable garden for some stills tomorrow.'

Salter consulted his notebook. 'Try Inigo

Robinson on Davenport,' he said. 'He specializes in gnomes.'

'How do you know?'

'It's just one of the things I know about,' Salter said. 'Now, about this weekend. You think I'm doing the right thing?'

'Oh yes, Charlie. You've never taken Angus or Seth away on their own. Don't worry about me. I need a weekend just to catch up.'

'Washing? Ironing?' Salter asked, surprised.

'No, at the studio. There's about six things going on and I'd like to get ahead of it if I can.'

'What will you do with Seth?'

'He's got a standing invitation to sleep over with his pal. Robbie. If not, I'll think of something. Now, did you get anywhere with the screen door yet?'

Salter picked up the paper. 'I'll phone Fred Staver. If he can't fix it, we may have to put the house up for sale.'

Annie recognized this for what it was, not an answer, but a flung gauntlet, and declined to pick it up.

CHAPTER THREE

He had arranged to interview Drecker's girlfriend, Julia Costa, at work since she was alone there in the mornings. The shop was called Mary Lightfoot Interiors without punctuation, and it specialized in 'collections'. There was an Indian collection along one wall, a collection of glass furniture that Drecker's assistant would have approved of filled the centre of the room, and the back of the shop was devoted to a bamboo collection. Five or six smaller collections were grouped about the store, including one from the west, of chairs in the shape of saddles, and an 'Old Ontario' collection of iron and copper fireplace implements grouped around a pine mantel. The idea, as far as Salter could see, was for the customer to have a different collection in every room of the house. The prices were all in units of a hundred dollars, written out in script.

The woman who came forward as Salter entered was in her middle thirties. She wore a denim skirt and a top made of knitted string. She seemed to have glass slippers through which her feet showed, but Salter presumed they were plastic. She was tall, with a slightly Irish look about her face and hair—a very pale skin with what Salter thought of as greenery-yallery eyes and a lot of dark hair twisted into a rough bunch behind.

Salter showed her his identification and she took him into a back room, leaving the door open so she could watch for customers.

'You want to know where Dennis was when the store burned down,' she said. 'He was with me.'

'You've been talking to him, of course.'

'Sure. He phoned last night. Shouldn't he have?'

'It doesn't matter.'

'Oh, I see. We could be in a conspiracy, of course.'

She seems nervous, Salter thought, but who doesn't when the inspector calls. 'But you aren't?' he asked.

'No. I think it was an accident, anyway.'

'Why?'

'Have you checked on Cy?'

'In what way?'

'You'll find out he's got a record. His last store burned down, too.'

'The Insurance Protection Bureau will come up with that one. You think he set this up?'

'I think it's likely and somehow he didn't get out of the way in time.'

Salter said nothing. The details of Drecker's death did not fit her idea, and yet she sounded genuinely convinced of it herself. He said, 'Let's get back to Dennis Nelson. Can you swear he was with you from one-fifteen onwards?'

'Yes, I can.' She leaned back and crossed her legs, looking at Salter.

Salter persisted. 'If he were sleeping on a sofa in the living-room—you have a sofa?— you wouldn't have known if he disappeared for a couple of hours, would you?'

'He wasn't on the sofa, he was in my bed, and I would have known. As a matter of fact he kept me awake for two hours talking about Jake, his boyfriend, before we went to sleep.'

'Miss Costa, Nelson says he's bisexual. Are you lovers, like?' Salter tried his friendly bumpkin voice.

'No. It would have been OK with me, but that's neither here nor there. We've never made love. He says it would spoil our relationship—silly twit. He's a sweetheart and I love him and it's not the first time we've spent the night together when he's been upset. But, no, we aren't lovers. He may be the best friend I've got, though. I don't think he *is* bisexual, more's the pity.'

'It doesn't make for a very strong alibi, does it?'

'I've just thought of something. Dennis came in a cab. Find the driver and you'll know he arrived at my place, won't you?'

'That seems to cover Nelson. What about you?'

'How do you mean?'

'I'm looking for motives, Miss Costa. I'm told you were connected with Drecker.'

'Who told you that?' she said sharply. 'Not Dennis?'

'No. You for one, when you called him Cy. And Mrs Drecker.'

'So; all right, we were connected.'

'His mistress?'

She didn't answer for a few minutes. Then: 'What's a mistress, Inspector?'

If this was a game, then Salter had a few minutes to play. 'The regular sexual partner of a man who is married?' he offered.

'Not bad. He doesn't have to be married, though, does he?' she said. 'What's the difference between a mistress and a lover?'

'Money, I guess.' It was now clear that Julia Costa was involved in some metaphorical throat-clearing.

'Then what's the difference between a

mistress and a whore?' she asked, just before Salter got to this one himself.

'Not much. They both peddle it for money, but the whore works a lot harder.'

'Choose your term, then. I had sex with Drecker about once every two weeks.'

'For money?'

'He gave me money, yes.'

'It sounds very businesslike. Did you like him?'

'Does it? Yes, I did. He was a handsome man, Inspector. Has anyone told you that? He looked like Clark Gable with wavy hair. And he enjoyed himself. He reminded me of a guy I knew in Saskatoon, a guy called Big Red. Big Red owned six cabs and he lost them one night in a crap game, but he didn't shoot himself. He just laughed and went back to driving one of his own cabs, with a little pimping on the side. For Saskatoon, that's style. Cy was like that. He was a bit of a crook, maybe, but he enjoyed himself. He liked winning on a deal, but he could lose, too. He liked women, and in Toronto that isn't all that common.'

'You mean that everyone you know here is gay?' Salter asked incredulously.

'No, just the opposite. The gays I know like women, but the others, the disco crowd

I've met, don't seem to. They want you, of course, but when they get you they don't seem to enjoy it much. They frighten easy, too. Cy didn't. He liked me.' She moved both hands up to adjust her hair at the back, lifting her breasts within the string vest. The gesture reminded Salter of a colleague in Homicide who liked to stand with one hand on his hip, holding back his jacket just enough so that the customers could see the butt of his gun.

'His wife doesn't share your opinion,' he said.

'His wife doesn't like sex,' Julia Costa said. 'They found that out early, back in the days when you had to get married to find out. But even *that* Cy didn't turn into a big deal. I think he married her because she held out on him, and when he realized what she was like, he just took the loss and found other women. She didn't care, and they got along well together. He said she was a smart businesswoman.'

'I see.' Salter the more-or-less contented husband had been appalled in his soul at the emptiness of Drecker's flat, the lack of food, warmth or sex, but as Julia Costa explained it, it sounded plausible that Drecker would not have cared. Another world.

104

'What about Nelson?' he asked. 'Drecker was pretty unpleasant to him, wasn't he?' He was having trouble with the image of Cyril Drecker, the salt of the earth.

'Not really. He teased him, is all. He liked Dennis, I think, but for Cy, Dennis was someone to have fun with. I'm not defending Cy, but he wasn't mean or vicious. If Dennis had laughed back and teased Cy about—oh, I don't know—something—he would have loved it. He was rough, a rough diamond, if you like, but no sadist.'

'If you are Dennis Nelson it must be hard to tell the difference,' Salter said, realizing that he was 'relating' to Nelson.

'I know,' she sighed. 'Poor Dennis. The only taboo subject we had was what I saw in Drecker.'

'What about his enemies—Drecker, I mean? Did you know of any?'

She shook her head. 'A lot of people didn't like him, but setting fire to his store would be too much. No.'

'Okay, Miss Costa. Now the rest of your story. You were by yourself until Nelson arrived?'

'Yes, I was. I was in bed when he arrived.'

'Did you get any phone calls during the evening?'

105

'Yes, I did. I got one about twelve-thirty.'

'Who from?'

'A man named Raymond Darling. He's married, by the way, so you might question him at his work.' Now she looked embarrassed. 'He *is* my lover. Nobody gets paid.'

'Where can I find him?'

'He has a little showroom on Church Street. He's a bathroom remodeller—a plumber, really.'

Salter noted the number. Darling, Julia Costa's lover, had remodelled the bathroom in Drecker's store. Afterwards, according to Dennis Nelson, Darling and Drecker had had a swearing match. Julia Costa must have heard of it. Save some for later, when she isn't ready for it, and list Darling as suspect number three.

'May I ask you where you met Raymond Darling, Miss Costa?'

'Through the trade,' she said promptly. 'I used to work in a store off Queen Street West, and Raymond was in and out all the time. He's interested in antiques.'

'Did you introduce him to Drecker?'

'Yes, I did.' She looked at Salter. 'That's *all* I did, Inspector. I told Drecker I knew a plumber, and I told Raymond that Drecker needed a bathroom fixed. After that they were on their own.'

Salter considered his next question carefully. 'Was there any chance,' he asked, 'that either man knew of your relationship with the other?'

'None. None at all. No way. Drecker knew I didn't belong to him exclusively. Raymond thinks I do—he wouldn't like the idea of sharing me. But they both knew that one word about me to anyone else and I would have made their life bloody hell. That was clear from the start—no confessions to wives—nothing. My life is private.'

'But it is possible that Darling, by chance, could have heard of your relationship with Drecker and taken action, become jealous, like?' He was goading her now.

'No. The only one who could have told him was Drecker himself. And Cy didn't need to boast.'

'Dennis Nelson knew about you and Drecker.'

She laughed. 'Don't you worry about Dennis, Inspector. He may not like Raymond, but he doesn't have a nasty bone in his body. My private life is a sacred trust with him.'

'One last thing, Miss Costa. When you and

107

Drecker got together, where was it usually?'

'Above the store, always. He liked that arrangement.'

'That's how Nelson knew of it?'

'No. Drecker told him. He liked to tease Dennis.'

Salter got up to go and she accompanied him to the door. As he was leaving, she said, 'One thing, Inspector. I need a favour.'

'I can guess. I won't talk to your boyfriend about you and Drecker if it isn't necessary.'

'Thanks.' She pushed the door open for him without looking at him. 'I still think it was an accident,' she said.

*   *   *

Salter put another quarter in the parking meter and walked through to The Cakemaster for coffee and a cheese Danish. On Saturdays Annie bought croissants here and they ate them heated up for breakfast on Sundays. For a special treat she bought cheese Danish, and Salter had become addicted to it. Whenever he was in the area (and working on his own) he tried to squeeze in a coffee break at The Cakemaster.

He gobbled one of the pastries and wiped the crumbs off his face and hands, and got out his notebook. He had now questioned all the main people in his list. The obvious suspects all had alibis, except for Raymond Darling who would have, he was sure, and that ended round one. Nobody with singed eyebrows had appeared, and no one was missing except Jake Hauser, Nelson's boyfriend, and the Japanese collector. Unless one of these was his man, it looked like a long and maybe hopeless case, a killing by person or persons unknown. Round two was a matter of endless patient questioning, of the neighbours again, of the suspects, and of anyone else even faintly connected with the dead man. There were searches to be done— of Drecker's store and his apartment. Someone would be assigned to watch the store to see if any strangers took an unusual interest in it. In all of this Salter would play second fiddle to the experts in Homicide, to the well-known team of Munnings and Hutter.

Salter let the waitress refill his cup. He had lots of time to see Darling before his squash game, and then he would let the Superintendent, Orliff, decide. Through the window of the café he saw a fleet of tow-trucks assemble to haul away illegally-parked cars on Cumberland Street. Already the policeman in charge was arguing with an owner who had appeared just as his car was being hoisted off its front wheels, ready to go to the pound, where it would cost the owner a small fortune to get it back. Salter watched the officer keeping his patience as the citizen, red in the face, danced about on the sidewalk, demanding his car back; but once the tow-truck was hitched up, the full fine and fees had to be paid.

'Dickens,' said a fat, smoothly-groomed man standing next to Salter.

It was Browne, the chairman of the English Department at Douglas College, the scene of a recent case Salter had been involved in.

'Hullo, Professor,' Salter said. 'What's Dickens got to do with tow-trucks?'

'*Our Mutual Friend,* Inspector. In Dickens's time, some watermen made a living scavenging bodies from the Thames and picking the pockets before they turned the corpses over to the authorities, who paid them a bounty. When bodies were in short supply, these ghouls were not above hiring murderers to supply them. Those tow-truck operators out there are the ghouls of our time.'

'Somebody has to be the scavenger. We don't enjoy it much either,' Salter said.

110

'Of course, of course. I was just getting off a nice literary analogy. I don't drive, myself. Nice to see you, Inspector.' He picked up his bill. 'I have to buy some Florentines for my daughter.'

Salter watched the girl pick out a dozen large, brown cookies, and hand them to the Professor.

'Try some,' Browne called from the cash register. 'They're *delicious*.'

All right, thought Salter, guessing from what he knew of Browne that you could trust him on cookies.

'I'll have a dozen of those,' he said, when he came to pay his bill. The girl put them in a bag and added up the tab.

'Twenty-five twelve,' she said.

Salter stared at her. 'Two dollars a *cookie?*' he asked.

'Two dollars a Florentine,' she corrected.

Salter put away the five-dollar bill and gave the girl two twenties. Bought a treat today, Annie, he rehearsed. A few cookies. Twenty-five dollars worth. Jesus Christ. Who says I'm tight?

★   ★   ★

The window of Darling's plumbing shop

displayed a small badly-made cardboard model of a bathroom; inside the store were several coloured bathroom fixtures, and the counter held advertising displays of faucets that could be installed by the home handyman. It looked as if Darling still needed to bring in the day-to-day cash while he moved up-market.

The man sitting behind the counter, reading the business section of *Globe and Mail*, was about forty years old, handsome, with a slight tan and fair, curly hair. His dark leather pants looked, to Salter's eye, several sizes too small, and his brown silk shirt (more like a blouse, the policeman thought) was open to show his chest and a large gold key on a chain. And this is what Annie and Jenny want me to look like? Salter inquired of himself.

'Raymond Darling?' he asked.

'That's me, friend,' the man said, and laid down his paper. He smiled to show a full set of white teeth with a large gap in the centre of the top row.

'You know who I am?'

'I can guess.'

'You don't have to, though, do you? Your girlfriend just phoned you.'

They were sparring. Darling was matching

his man-of-the-world 'cool' with Salter's tweed jacket and short haircut.

Salter let him have his hour. 'I understand, Mr Darling, that the night before last you telephoned Miss Costa, at her apartment. Could you tell me the time of the call? Just a routine check.' There. The flat-footed cop to the life.

Darling rose like a hungry bass. 'I called Miss Costa at twelve-thirty from a friend's house,' he said, the words uninflected as they would be under cross-examination.

'You are close friends with Miss Costa?'

'Very close.' Darling smiled around the court-room.

'Lovers, I understand.'

Darling smiled again.

Then Salter, still playing the flat-foot, let him have it. 'I understand that you and Cyril Drecker got into an argument last week. You were shouting threatening remarks, I believe. What was that all about, could you tell me?'

'Nelson told you that, did he?'

Salter waited. Just answer the question, Mr Darling.

'It was nothing at all. I did some work for Drecker, and he didn't want to pay for it. He was a bit of a shafter. Has anyone told you that?'

113

'I see.' Salter pretended to write it all down. This is fun, he thought. 'A disagreement over a bill?'

'Right.'

'That looks after Miss Costa, then.' Salter wrote away busily.

'Good.' Darling shook out his paper again.

'What was the job you did for Mr Drecker?' Salter asked, licking his thumb and turning to a fresh page of his notebook.

'I put in the bathroom on the second floor of his store, designed it for him. I'm a qualified plumber, but I do a lot of design work now. Some friends, a lawyer and a doctor friend of mine, want to put up the money for me to expand as soon as I find a better location. But I knew Drecker as a dealer, too. I do a bit of dealing myself. Here.' He came round the counter and led the way into a back area, formerly a plumbing workshop. Now most of the space was taken up with furniture that was being stripped. 'I know a fair bit about antiques,' he said.

Salter looked at a collection of bits and pieces of rubbish that even Drecker might have been ashamed of. 'Very interesting. Now where were you that night?'

'Me? I was at a poker game with some

friends. It's a regular game. Mostly professional people.'

'I see. What time did you get home?'

'About half past one.'

'Your wife could confirm this?'

'I think so.' Now Darling looked smug. 'You want to ask her? Here.' He gave Salter a card printed with 'Raymond Darling— Bathroom and Kitchen Designs'. 'My home address is on the back.'

Salter took the card and prepared to leave.

'Oh, Inspector,' Darling said, 'I'd be grateful if you didn't tell my wife about the phone call.' He put a hand on Salter's arm. 'She'd be upset by Julia.'

'Nothing to do with us, Mr Darling,' Salter said, the bumpkin again. 'I just want to confirm the movements of everyone who might have had reason to commit the crime.'

'Good. Thanks. Must be a rotten job yours, sometimes.' The decline from braggart to chumminess, via defensiveness, was complete.

Salter nodded stolidly and left. Darling had impressed him as almost fitting Julia Costa's description of Cyril Drecker: Tom Jones with his wits about him. Was it a type she attracted or did she go looking for this kind of man?

Darling's house was in Cabbagetown, the new, fashionable Cabbagetown that was taking over the old working-class district. No. 23 was in the process of having its porch removed and its front yard cobbled. Salter knocked and waited. Just as he was about to knock again, a small dark haired woman wheeling a baby carriage turned into the yard. She was in her mid-thirties, with a hard-looking little body dressed in sweatshirt and jeans which showed the muscles of her thighs. Her face was cheerful with the look of someone who enjoyed a joke, and she crackled with energy as she manouevred the carriage into the front yard and leaped back in mock surprise at seeing Salter on the doorstep. 'Don't tell me,' she cried. 'You're selling aluminium siding. Right?'

'No, ma'am.'

'Roofing?'

Salter shook his head.

'Real estate? You want to list the house?'

'I'm from the police, ma'am,' Salter said. 'May I come in?'

'Oh Jesus, yes. What have I done?'

'Nothing that I know of. I want to ask a

116

few questions about your husband's acquaintances. He's done nothing either,' he added quickly. Across the street, five bums from the old Cabbagetown were watching him from the broken-down porch of an unreconstructed hovel. *They* had certainly smelt him for what he was. Mrs Darling lifted her baby out of its carriage and unlocked the door, and they went into the living-room. Here Darling's avocation was everywhere apparent. The room was a junk heap of bits and pieces of furniture. There were three rocking-chairs, a grandfather clock, and a huge wardrobe without doors, as well as assorted tables and ornaments.

'Mrs Darling, I have to confirm the movements of everyone who might have been involved in an incident that happened the night before last.'

Mrs Darling laid the baby on one of the chairs and stared at Salter, with her hand flat on her breast, over-reacting as she seemed to do to everything.

'Your husband isn't involved, but he has confirmed the whereabouts of a couple of people and we want to get the times straight.'

'The people he was playing poker with? They are all professional people,' she said, echoing the husband.

Salter ignored this. 'Can you confirm the time your husband came home?'

'Just a minute, Officer. This little bugger has done it again. Let me change him and I'll be with you.' With expert bustle she stripped the baby of his wet diaper and folded a clean one. The baby waved his legs in the air and shouted happily at her. 'Now watch it, you little bastard,' she cried, tickling him. She turned to Salter. 'When I was changing him this morning, the little bugger pee'd straight in my eye,' she explained. She finished changing him, gave a final tickle, and put the baby on the floor.

'Now,' she said, sitting down in the chair herself. She looked hard at Salter, seeming to suppress a laugh. 'Twenty past one,' she said.

'Can you be certain?'

'You betcha. We have a clock beside the bed. Raymond pointed out the time, the way he always does.'

'You mean he announces the time every night when he gets into bed?'

'No,' she giggled. 'Afterwards.' She whooped and covered her mouth in mock seriousness.

'After what?' Salter asked cautiously, knowing the answer.

'After we do it.' She watched Salter's face

joyfully.

'I see. You mean you woke up when he came in and—made love?'

'We always do when he wins. He gets very excited when he wins and it calms him down,' she said, grinning again.

'I see. He came home and woke you up, you made love, and then you checked the time. Which was?'

'Quarter to two.' Another whoop. 'He was proud of himself. He said we had been doing it for twenty-five minutes.'

Salter was absorbed. I must remember to tell Annie about this, he thought. 'Did he always time himself?' he asked.

'It was a joke he started when we were first married.'

Salter resisted the temptation to ask what Darling's best time was. 'Well, that's that, then,' he said.

'Good,' replied a voice from behind him. It was Darling. 'Found out what you wanted to know?' He winked at his wife.

'Yes, thanks. I won't be troubling you again,' Salter said, touching his forehead with his finger.

'Care for a beer, Inspector, before you go? I've got some Stella Artois in the fridge.'

'No, thanks. I must be getting back,'

Salter said, and started to leave. The Darlings followed him, grinning, to the door.

Stella Artois, for Christ's sake, he thought. What was that? Some Greek beer professional people drink?

But, to his ear, Darling's wife was telling the naked, vulgar truth, which confirmed the alibis of the two people closest to Drecker, his mistress and his assistant.

When Salter returned to his office, Gatenby was already waiting to report. 'I did the list,' the Sergeant said. 'Some of these places—you should have seen them! Fagin would be ashamed to own them. I asked them all what they knew about Drecker, what dealings they had with him, but I couldn't smell anything fishy. All the same story: the high class ones bought the odd things from Drecker to sell again, and the real grungy ones that were full of old toot...' He pronounced the word to rhyme with 'put'.

'Old what?'

'Old toot. What my old mum used to call it. Rubbish.'

'Go on.'

'They used to sell their rubbish to him if he thought he could make something on it.'

'So that's that, then.'

'Ah no. No. Something very interesting

120

cropped up. About half of these shops, mostly the good ones, told me about an old Japanese chap who'd been looking for anything they had recently bought from Drecker.' Gatenby sat, shining, waiting to be prodded on.

'You mean after you'd asked them about Drecker, half of these people said, "There was an old Japanese in here last week asking after him?"' Salter said patiently.

'No, no. It happened with the first one, a dealer in pine on Avenue Road. He told me about the Japanese fella. So I asked the next one, and he'd had this guy in, too. I knew you'd be interested so after that I asked them all. Eight of the fourteen confirmed they'd had a Japanese inquiring about anything Drecker sold them.' Gatenby paused.

Salter waited to be sure the story was over, then said, 'So what do you think, Frank? Have we got a Maltese Falcon on our hands?'

'What, in Toronto?' Gatenby gaped.

'I'm joking,' Salter said. 'But who is this old guy?'

'Ah,' Gatenby said. 'I'm not finished yet. Vancouver phoned. They haven't found Gene Tanabe and there's no one been fished out of the harbour lately, but they had something else to tell us. Seems your

Japanese friend was inquiring himself about three weeks ago after someone else, someone called George Kemp that he knew forty years ago in Vancouver.'

'Did they know him? This Kemp?'

'No. But I asked them to check up on him for *us* if they could. They'll phone us back.'

'You've been busy, Frank. Anything else?'

'The chief wants to see you.'

'Okay. Anything else? Maybe I can hold the chief off until you've got this one all wrapped up.'

Gatenby grinned. 'Better not. He's called down twice. I'll proceed with inquiries, as they say, while you keep him happy.'

'That's it, then? No bumf today?'

'Lots, but I sent it all back. They wanted you to talk to the cadets about police administration. Then there's that programme where the schoolkids take over a station for the day—could you organize that? I told them, no. And—oh yes—would you be available to brief the new members of the Police Commission about our work. I said we were too busy right now, and to tell the commissioners to come back next year. A lot of little stuff, too, but I took care of it.'

'You're a treasure, Frank. I have a feeling we'll be a few more days yet, so keep them at bay. I'll go and see Orliff.'

★   ★   ★

The Superintendent was in his office, and Salter gave him what he had so far.

'Couldn't have been an accident?'

'The Fire Marshall doesn't think so.'

Orliff made a note. 'So far, then, you've got six possibilities: the assistant, his friend, the girlfriend, the wife, this Darling character, and the old Japanese. The assistant and the girlfriend could have done it together, couldn't they? They sound like a flakey pair.'

'She had nothing against Drecker that I know of.'

'What do you make of her, though, and the assistant?'

'Nothing much. The assistant is all right. He's uptight but he's quarrelling with his boyfriend. There might be something there, when I find the boyfriend. The woman is nervous about something, but she didn't seem like a killer to me. If you want *my* preference, it would be for this guy Darling.'

'Why?'

'He's a cocky bastard, and I think Drecker might have swindled him. Darling wouldn't like that.'

'But he's got an alibi, Charlie, as good as any of the others.'

'I guess so.' Salter shrugged.

Orliff looked at Salter for a long minute until Salter looked away.

'So what are you going to do now?' Orliff asked.

'Talk to this lot again. See if I can smell anything else. Find Nelson's boyfriend, and the Japanese. It could be I haven't picked up anything real yet.'

'That's what I was thinking. You haven't got much in the way of motives, have you? What about the wife? She takes over the store, and I guess there's insurance. Could she have hired someone to do it?'

Salter shrugged again. 'I can't figure her out. She could be the head guard in a women's concentration camp, or one of those people who don't kill mosquitoes because all life is sacred. Her relationship with Drecker was pretty strange, and I couldn't get much idea of her life away from him, except that she spends a lot of time on yoga and bridge.'

Orliff made another note. 'Okay, stay with it next week. After that we'll let the Homicide people have it. Let Munnings and Hutter beat their brains out. All right,

Charlie. No real suspects, no motives, no clues. Don't make yourself ill. Something will turn up.' Orliff nodded in dismissal. Just then his telephone rang. Salter got up to go but Orliff signalled him back. 'It's for you,' he said.

It was Gatenby. 'Vancouver on the phone,' he said immediately. 'Do you want to talk to them?'

'Yes. What extension?'

'Two-o-five.'

Salter pressed the button. 'Salter here. Who am I talking to?'

'Sergeant don't-make-any-jokes Renfrew. We've found your man.'

'Tanabe?'

'No. Kemp.'

'Christ, that's quick. I thought he'd left town forty years ago.'

'You know how it is sometimes. This country's just one big village strung out along the forty-ninth parallel. We called the union hall—your man was a steam-fitter—and they asked around among the old-timers and someone remembered him. He lived in Victoria until six months ago—they even knew his address—and the local post office gave us his forwarding address. He lives in Woodstock, Ontario, now. Here's the address.'

'Great. Many thanks. No sign of Tanabe?'

'No. He owns an antique store on Pandora Street here in town. His assistant—a gorgeous Japanese piece, by the way—is very worried about him. He called her from Toronto last week, but since then they've heard nothing.'

'Family?'

'He doesn't have one. Parents dead. No brothers or sisters. Not married.'

'Anything known?'

'Nothing. Totally clean.'

'Right. Thanks again.' Salter hung up and turned to Orliff.

'The old Japanese is still missing, but we've got a lead on the guy *he* was looking for.'

'Something to do, anyway, Charlie,' Orliff said equably. 'Lotsa luck.'

Back in his office, Salter phoned the town police at Woodstock and told them who he was looking for. A car was despatched, the neighbours were talked to, and in half an hour the Woodstock police were calling him back.

'He doesn't live here any more,' the sergeant reported. 'He moved last month to Toronto.' He gave an address in the Beaches district. 'The neighbours think he's living with his daughter there. By the way, there's something else a little strange. The neighbours told us that another guy was in town last week trying to find Kemp...'

'... An old Japanese?'

'I guess so. They said Chinese, but all they know is oriental. You know about him?'

'I keep crossing his trail, as the mounties say. He's the one I'm really looking for.'

'Is he, though? Well, good luck. I expect that completes the Woodstock phase of your investigation, Inspector?'

Salter laughed and hung up. He looked at his watch. 'I'm going out to get a sandwich, Frank', he said. 'Then I'm going over to find this guy Kemp. He might lead me to Tanabe. We are missing two guys—Tanabe and Nelson's boyfriend, Hauser. If either of them comes by, put him on a hook until I get back. I'll call in after I've seen this Kemp, but I won't come back unless there's something to do here. I have to go to the hospital this afternoon.'

'Again? What for?'

'I don't know.' Salter jerked at his tie. 'If I ask them they won't tell me. "X-rays," they said. "What for?" I asked. "To establish a diagnosis for the probable cause of

127

microscopic hæmaturia," they said. "What's that?" I said? "You are peeing blood," they said. That's where I started.'

'That's what they do nowadays. They give you tests, look up the results on a computer and tell you what you've got. If they're wrong, they tell you the computer malfunctioned. I'm sure it's nothing.'

'It sure drags on, though,' Salter said as he left to find George Kemp.

★   ★   ★

Kemp's daughter lived in the Beaches, an area in the east end where the city and the lake meet in a way that makes it possible for the local citizens to enjoy Toronto's only natural amenity. There is a park here, beside the lake, and a boardwalk that runs along the shore, and in July, if the wind is in the right direction so that it doesn't bring in waves from the permanently frigid waters in the centre of Lake Ontario—waters so cold that there is a legend that sailors who drown never come to the surface—it is possible to swim, for a week or two, anyway.

Like a lot of Toronto people, Salter was sentimental about the Beaches. He had grown up nearby and spent large parts of his

128

school holidays on the beach. His father still lived in the area, in a small flat not far from the streetcar barns where he had worked all his life, and Salter was always glad when his route took him through the area.

Since Salter's boyhood, other parts of the lakefront had been made accessible to the population. 'Harbourfront' had been born, a centre of cultural and social activity drawing crowds year round, especially on sweltering summer nights. But the Beaches is a real district, where people live, the most human quarter of the city.

Salter drove down Jarvis Street and eastwards along Queen to the race track, then south and east again to run along the edge of the park until he came to Melita Street. He cruised slowly, looking for the number he wanted, noting that while the street was still apparently intact, with the same small family homes, many of them owned or rented by the kind of people Salter had grown up with, some brightly-painted verandas testified to the arrival of new immigrants from the Mediterranean. Here and there, too, the white-painters had appeared, sandblasting their way across the city in the name of restoration.

Salter found his house, parked, and

knocked on the door. A small, fat, frizzy-haired woman in her forties opened it. Over her shoulder Salter could see down the hall into the kitchen where a man of the same age was reading a paper.

'Mrs Murdrick?'

'Yes?' the woman said in a no-thank-you tone.

Salter showed his identification. 'I'd like to talk to you about your father,' he said.

'Oh, I don't know. What about? Phil!' she called to her husband over her shoulder, keeping her eye on Salter.

Her husband looked up. 'What?' he shouted in a don't-keep-bothering-me voice.

'There's a policeman here asking about Dad.'

'You'd better ask him in then, hadn't you?'

Salter stepped into the hallway.

'What's the trouble?' Murdrick asked, a man who knew his rights.

'No trouble. I'm looking for George Kemp,' Salter said.

'Well, yez've found him,' a voice said from the top of the stairs. An old man stood on the landing, short, barrel-chested with stubby legs and long arms. His face was brick-red and shiny, and his lower jaw was thrust forward, giving him an aggressive look. A pair of old-fashioned steel-rimmed glasses had worn a groove in the bridge of his nose.

Slowly, rolling from side to side, he descended the stairs until he came face to face with Salter. 'George Kemp,' he said.

'I'm making inquiries about a Mr Gene Tanabe,' Salter said. 'I think you know him.'

'Ah,' Kemp said. He cleared his throat with a sound like a drain being unplugged, blew his nose in a large khaki handkerchief, adjusted his glasses, and waited.

For a few moments no one spoke or moved. Then Kemp turned and started to walk back up the stairs. 'You'd better come up here,' he said.

Salter looked at Mr and Mrs Murdrick, who said nothing, so he followed the old man up the stairs and into his room. Kemp was already seated in an armchair by the window.

'Close the door,' he said. 'We 'ave no particler need to let his majesty—,' he pointed with a stumpy finger to the floor— 'know all our business.'

Salter closed the door and sat down in the other chair.

Kemp said, 'I take me meals with me daughter, but I spend me time up here when I'm at home. I can make meself a cup of tea, and it avoids too much argumenting.' His accent Salter had now placed as Newfoundland—round Irish vowels drained of their music, and a slightly ornate syntax.

'I don't know where Gene is to be found at this particler moment,' Kemp began. 'But I do know him, yes. I've known him ever since I first came to Canada.'

'You aren't Canadian?' Slater asked, puzzled.

'I am, mister, but I was born in Newfoundland, and in them days we wasn't part of Canada. When I left in nineteen hundred and forty-two we still wasn't. But before I tell the whole history, would yez like a cup of tea? Yez'll have to take it bare-legged, because I'm not allowed to drink milk, the doctor says.'

Salter declined and looked around while the old man made himself a cup of black tea. The room was furnished so that a single person could look after himself. There was a washbasin in one corner, a two-burner hotplate on a small metal table, a single bed, a bureau, and several well-worn rugs.

Kemp organized himself in his armchair and began again.

'I met him first in nineteen forty-two in Vancouver, where I was working on a government contract.'

'You were a steam-fitter?'

'I was and am a Master Steam-Fitter and a Master Plumber,' Kemp said. 'When I took me apprenticeship in Newfoundland, you got your papers for both.' He stopped, inviting Salter to question or comment on the story so far.

Salter recognized that Kemp was one of those people who could not tell a story simply, but required to be prodded along each step of the way. A tedious business.

'And you went to Vancouver when you got your papers?' he asked, trying for a small leapfrog.

But Kemp wasn't to be abbreviated. 'not right away, I didn't,' he said. 'I had me own business in St John's at first. I borryed a bit of money from the bank, d'ye see, and bought out old Murdoch McElway's shop. It was going downhill and I got it cheap.'

A long pause. Salter started to get a little fed up. He waited forever—two minutes? three?—and opened his mouth to speak some words of encouragement. But the ancient plumber was now fully embarked on his tale, and the story came in larger chunks.

'When the war came, business fell off, so I went to work for the government, in Canada. I'd never been west of Halifax, and I took a chance and went out to Vancouver. I says to the wife, we might never get the opportunity again, and she agreed. So the finish was that I installed heating plants in about half the army camps in British Columbia. After the war I went up north to the D.E.W. Line, Distant Early Warning Line, that was, and after that I went to work for the oil companies all over Alberta. I'm known in the trade everywhere west of Winnipeg and east of Halifax, and the only province I've never set foot in is Quebec. I never bothered with this part of the country until me wife died two years ago. I was in Victoria then, and I stayed there about a year and then packed up and came down east to be near to me daughter and him as she's married to.' Once again Kemp pointed with contempt to the floor where the sound of the Murdricks' quarrelling could be heard through the floorboards.

'You moved to Woodstock?'

'Ah. That was near enough to be able to see her occasionally. I was retired, of course, but I bought a little house and started to do a few odd jobs, working for the hardware store nearby. Pretty soon I was as busy as a one-armed paperhanger. These Ontario fellas don't seem to know how to put a bit of glass in a window, nor a washer on a tap. A man who's built his own house can always make a livin'. I never went short of something to do once they found out about me. I've always kept me licence and me truck, though I never thought I'd end up as a hobbler.'

I wonder if he can fix a screen door, thought Salter. Just then, there was a timid tap at the door and Kemp's face split into a huge smile.

'Come in, young fella!' he called.

The door opened and Salter gaped at a tiny George Kemp who stood in the doorway holding on to the doorknob which was almost level with his eye. Salter looked close and saw a small boy, five or six years old, dressed in a miniature version of Kemp's overalls, with a small lunch-pail in his hand. Even the tiny steel-rimmed glasses were the same. Behind them, though, was a pale, diffident face which stared shyly at Salter.

'Come in and meet the polis,' Kemp said, accenting the first syllable.

The boy edged forward.

'Inspector,' Kemp said, 'this is me helper, George, named after me. Me grandson,' he added proudly. 'George, this is Inspector Salter. Shake hands with him like I showed you. I'm teaching him some manners,' he added to Salter.

And driving your daughter up the wall, Salter thought, as he solemnly shook hands with the boy.

'George comes out on me rounds,' Kemp said, his red face glowing. 'It didn't take me long to find a hardware store here with a use for me services, and this young man and I have a few calls to make today. Now, young fella, you've got your lunch, have you? He allus brings his lunch to eat in the truck with me,' he said to Salter. 'Well, I won't be long. You go down and wait in the truck and I'll be right down.'

He watched as the child obediently left the room, carefully closing the door with his eyes on Kemp to see if he was noticing how well he did it.

'That's the main reason I stay here,' Kemp said, when the door was shut. 'The lad needs me to teach him a few things.'

After a respectful pause, Salter prompted him to continue his story. 'What happened after Woodstock?' he asked.

'I took sick. I incurred an infarction of me heart,' the old man said. 'They thought I was going to die, but they was wrong shipped on that one. I pulled through. But then me daughter insisted I come up here to be with her because the doctors said I shouldn't be left to meself. Three weeks I was on the critical list.' He paused to give weight to his next words. 'And that is why you are talking to me at this moment now,' he said.

Salter waited. After another pause, he asked, 'Why is that, Mr Kemp?'

'Because *that* was when Gene's box went.'

At last, Gene Tanabe's box. 'How?' Salter asked. 'How did it go?'

'That is the bloody mystery I'd like *you* to get to the bottom of, mister. I'd had that box for forty years, and when I come out of hospital it was gone.'

'Why? Why did you have it?'

'I had it because Gene Tanabe trusted me with it. I looked after it for forty years and when I got sick for the first time in me life, it went.' The old man spoke with a solemn passion, as though he had been over the words again and again in his mind, learning them by heart.

'Gene Tanabe was a friend of yours?'

'He was and is. I never let him down. He knows that. At least he knows the box went unbeknownst to me.'

Salter tried again. Each end of the story was important.

'Could we go back to the beginning, Mr Kemp? Why did he leave the box with you?'

'Because you fellas, the polis, came for him and took him away. You thought he was a dangerous enemy alien. He wouldn't hurt a bloody fly, mister.'

'He was interned?' Salter asked, ignoring Kemp's detour into Tanabe's innocence.

'They all was. Interned. Shipped away. It was no place to be Japanese in nineteen forty-two, Vancouver wasn't.'

'So he trusted you with a box of his possessions?'

'That's right. We was neighbours. He was a woodworker, did you know? He could do anything with wood. He made me a tool-box you could bury a baby in—beautiful bit of work—but the nicest thing he made that I saw was a doll's house for me little girl. She's still got it. I'm pretty handy with metal meself, and when we got to know each other we used to swap little jobs. I did all the plumbing around his house and the odd bit of solderin' and such, and he did all the joinery I needed doing. He was a lovely fella. When they told him he had to move, he come to me and says would I look after this box for him. A good thing, too, because he lost everything else in the finish, commandeered by the local patriots. I was glad to help out. It was a privilege, mister, to do something for him.'

'Then what happened? After the war he came back to look for you?' Salter asked, still keeping his distance from Mr Kemp's belligerent sentimentalism.

'That's right. But we was gone. There was a fire at our house, d'ye see, and we had to move. When he come back to look for me, I was gone. He tells me now he figured that the box went in the fire. It didn't, you know. I still had it with me, but he stopped looking then.'

'Why didn't you try and find him?'

'Do you think I bloody didn't?' Kemp shouted suddenly, angry at being accused of leaving a stone unturned. 'I went back to the district dozens of times after the war, but he never came back from Ontario until nineteen forty-seven or 'eight, and by that time I'd given up traipsin' around looking for him. I told Gene I'd keep the box safe, and safe it was, with me.' Then in a conversational tone, he added, 'Tell you the truth, I thought he might be a goner by then.'

'But you kept the box. Did you know what was in it?'

'I kept the box, yes, and no, I did not know what was in it until last week. It wasn't none of my business.'

'Last week?' Now the other end of the
139

story was coming into sight.

'Ah. When Gene come back here. He'd tracked me down, d'ye see, found out where I was and knocked on the door. I didn't recognize him at first. Then, when I did realize it was Gene, the first thing I thought, o'course, was how I didn't have his box. It wasn't like it was supposed to be.'

'Did he think you still had the box?'

Kemp shook his head. 'No, mister, he knew I didn't. He'd found his box by then as well as some of his pictures. He said he just couldn't understand how they'd appeared like that, sudden-like, but he knew there would be a good reason and he only wanted to find out what it was. He trusted me from start to finish. And so he should. If I hadn't gone into hospital, I would have his box safe still.'

'But he wouldn't know that, would he, Mr Kemp?'

'Mebbe not. I would, though,' Kemp said. He took his glasses off, blew his nose, and wiped his face off before putting his glasses back on.

'What *did* he think?' Salter asked.

'Nothing. He didn't jump to conclusions, just waited to hear my story. After he heard about how the box disappeared while I was in hospital, he didn't care any more. Or p'raps I should say that he was so pleased to find I hadn't let him down after forty years that the box didn't interefere with our enjoyments if you understand me.'

Salter nodded.

'We went out for a bit of supper then,' Kemp continued. 'He took me to a place downtown—we went by taxicab—where we had a slap-up Japanese dinner.' Kemp's manner became diffident. 'You ever had a Japanese dinner?' he asked.

Salter shook his head.

'A bit peculiar,' Kemp said. 'Very *interestin'*, but not quite my cup of tea. Nice for a change, though, and they didn't make me sit cross-legged. They had a few proper tables. And Japanese beer is all right, so we had a few jars and got caught up. Old Gene has done wonderful well since I saw him last, and I've not done so bad, either. I tell you, mister, that evening with Gene was the best thing that's happened to me since I moved down east.' Kemp blew his nose again.

Salter waited a moment, and said, 'That was it, then? He found out it wasn't your fault, and that's the last you saw of him?'

'Not quite. He came back once more to say he'd got most of his pictures back. I came in

141

one day and found him talking to me son-in-law in the kitchen. The four of us had a drink together then, me and Gene and me daughter and that nunny-fudger she's married to, and that's the last I saw of him. He had to pay a terrible price to get his pictures, but he's a pretty rich man by all accounts, so no doubt he's happy on balance. Now, mister. I know how youse fellas' minds run so don't be thinking that Gene set fire to that shop out of revenge or something. It just isn't in him to do a thing like that.'

'Why has he disappeared, then?'

'How the hell do I know? P'raps he's afraid of you fellas—he has reason to be. But Gene Tanabe never hurt another human being in his life. You'll track him down eventually, I suppose, but I won't hold me breath waiting.'

Salter put away his notebook. 'Thanks, Mr Kemp. Can I find you here if I need you?'

'At mealtimes, I'm down below. The rest of the time, I'm here, or out doin' jobs. Now you can go down and confirm me account with me daughter.' Kemp stared triumphantly at Salter to show he knew how the police worked.

Salter stood up and then remembered. 'You haven't told me yet how the box disappeared,' he said.

'Ah, right. When I was in hospital with me infarction, me daughter sold me house and everything in it except for one or two bits she kept for this room here. They had a garage sale, d'ye see, and though she was particler to keep the box back, it went during the sale—lost, stolen, or strayed.'

'Do you think it might have been sold by mistake?'

'No. Me son-in-law conducted the sale.'

Salter waited, but there was no more forthcoming. Kemp sat, finished, staring out of the window.

On his way down, Salter passed the grandson sitting on the stairs, his lunch-pail at the ready, waiting for the policeman to let his playmate go.

Downstairs, Salter asked the Murdricks to confirm the essential points of Kemp's story.

'That's right. We think it must have been lifted during the sale,' the husband said. He sounded edgy, and his wife's next comment accounted for it.

'Forty years Dad kept that box. And as soon as his back was turned it was gone,' she said, giving her husband a look. It was evidently a line she had used before.

'It wasn't my bloody fault,' Murdrick answered. 'It was there the night before and

143

then it was gone. I didn't sell it. It was lifted, I tell you.'

Salter waited for an explanation.

'Phil was supposed to set aside the stuff Dad might want to keep, any mementoes, like, including the box, but when we went to pick them up after the sale, the box was gone,' she said.

'So you think someone stole it during the sale?'

'Must have,' Murdrick said. 'Must have. I was collecting the money, but I couldn't be everywhere, could I. Someone walked off with it.'

'Forty years,' his wife repeated.

'For Christ's sake don't keep on about it,' Murdrick said. 'The bloody thing wasn't worth a pinch of coon-shit.'

'Was anything in it?' Salter asked.

'Rubbish,' Murdrick said. 'Jap rubbish. Fans and pictures—all rubbish.'

'You don't know that, Phil.'

'I bloody well *do* know that,' he shouted. 'You had a look at the stuff. A pile of crap.'

'Was it locked?' Salter asked.

The wife blushed.

'Yes, it was,' Murdrick said. 'We opened it to find out if there was a name inside. I took the screws off. I closed it up again, and we

144

didn't touch anything.'

'I saw to that,' Mrs Murdrick said.

'Did you know why your father kept it?'

'He said he'd promised to keep it until Mr Tanabe returned.'

'Not likely after forty years, was it?' Salter said comfortingly, addressing himself to Murdrick. 'And yet he did. What a pity he didn't get there a bit sooner.'

'That's what I told him,' Mrs Murdrick agreed.

'When was it he came here?' Salter asked.

'Last week. He knew we didn't have the box any more, but he wanted to hear what happened. Funny, though, he didn't seem upset. More interested in talking to Dad, he was.'

'That was the only time you saw him?'

'No. He came back once more. He wanted to speak to Phil.'

'He was still nagging away about his bloody box,' Murdrick said. 'I told him to stop bothering us.'

'You were terrible to him,' his wife said, continuing the old row between them. 'There was no need to speak to him like that.'

'We did have a few words about it,' Murdrick said to Salter. 'But we all had a drink before he left.'

145

'He was a friend of Dad's and there was no need for you to treat him like that,' she said directly to her husband. They were ignoring Salter now.

'We fought those bastards during the war and I don't like them,' Murdrick shouted.

'Not you, you didn't. You didn't fight anyone. Anyway, no one had to fight Mr Tanabe. They put him in a concentration camp.'

Salter watched them argue.

'You keep on,' Murdrick threatened, 'and I'll do the same thing I did last time.'

'Go out and get—' she paused and looked at Salter—'pissed.'

'Go somewhere for some peace,' Murdrick corrected.

The two sat there simmering, and Salter judged that he had heard everything of any use to him. 'If you hear from him again, let me know, will you?' he said mildly.

There was no reply.

Salter added, 'And if I have any more questions, I suppose I can find you here, can I?' He looked inquiringly at Murdrick. What was he doing home at this time on a working day?

'My wife is always here. I might be out on a job but she'll take a message.'

'Where do you work, Mr Murdrick?'

'I work for myself. I'm a tiler.'

'Roofer?'

'No. *Not* a bloody roofer. Ceramics, mosaics—floors, bathrooms, fireplaces, I do all kinds of work, all quality work.'

'And you use this as your business phone?'

'That's right,' Murdrick said. 'It's legal. You can find me here.'

Salter got up to go and Mrs Murdrick led him out of the hall. 'I'm sorry about Mr Tanabe's box,' she said as she opened the front door for him. 'It's a shame after forty years.'

As she closed the door, Salter heard her husband shouting at her again from the kitchen.

★　　★　　★

'Slip this on, Mr Salter, and wait until we call you. Leave your clothes in the cubicle there and keep your shoes on.' A young Lena Horne imitating a nursing aide showed Salter to a changing booth where he did as he was told. He emerged in a white shroud that stopped at his knees and was missing the ties that held it together. Clutching it over his nakedness, he shuffled to the bench in his unlaced shoes like an inmate in a Dickensian madhouse. Two other men his own age were already sitting there, but the three men ignored each other for fear, in Salter's case, of learning what they were in for.

This was a hospital, so Salter had prepared himself for a wait of anything up to three hours by bringing a book, but he was surprised after a few minutes by the return of Lena Horne.

'Come with me, please,' she ordered, and led him down a long corridor to a small room with an X-ray table. 'Use the step and lie down on that,' she said. 'The technician will be here in a moment.'

Lena Horne gave way to Doris Day. 'Hi there,' she said. 'Let's have a look at you.'

Salter sat up and started to take off his shroud, and she leaped to stop him. 'That's all right,' she said. 'We can manage with that on.'

Salter lay back. He had so nerved himself up to the probable necessity of displaying his parts to all the female staff that he was now slightly disappointed. Once he had thought his fear of exposure in hospitals private and aberrant, but a sergeant of detectives had told him years before that if ever he, the sergeant, needed any kind of surgery below the neck he

148

would announce on entering the hospital that he would shave himself, thanks, and remind every shift of it until the operation was due.

'Could you move down a fraction—a bit more—that's it. Comfortable?'

'No.' A steel bar creased Salter's calf muscles instead of supporting his feet. Doris jiggled the support, moving it an inch.

'Better?' she asked.

'No,' he said. 'It hurts.' He had decided that this time he would not lie around smiling and uncomplaining until someone happened to notice that he was dying. He would be one of those surly bastards who survived.

'There isn't much I can do,' Doris Day said. 'You're pretty big.'

'I'm five feet ten and a half and I weigh a hundred and sixty-five pounds. About average. I can't lie with this thing under my legs for more than two minutes. How long do the X-rays take?'

'The doctor will be along shortly,' she said. 'Perhaps I could wrap a towel around it.'

'You do that,' Salter said.

She disappeared, and Salter heard her complaining about him to Lena Horne, but when she returned she was carrying a thing like a head-rest on two small rods. She removed the bar under his legs and replaced it with the padded rest. It was evidently designed for the job.

'All right, now?' she asked, as if she had laid Salter on a bed of swansdown but still expected him to complain.

'Perfect,' Salter said. 'Now if you'd turn on that light, I'll read until the doctor comes.'

'He'll be here *very* shortly,' she said.

'Good. When he comes, I'll stop reading.'

Reluctantly she turned on the light and went for the doctor. Once again Salter settled down for a long wait, and arranged himself so that he was not touching any of the icy chromium bars. Once again the technique worked, and Doris Day reappeared, accompanied by Richard Chamberlain, in need of a shave.

'This is Dr Tannenbaum,' she said.

The doctor nodded to him and fiddled with a hypodermic. 'This injection I'm going to give you will make you feel very cold, then very hot.' He paused. 'That's normal. But you could have an abnormal reaction. Are you allergic to anything?'

'Penicillin and euromycin,' Salter said. Simultaneously the doctor said something to the technician, and she started swabbing his arm.

He didn't hear me, thought Salter. I am

going to die.

'Now,' the doctor said, when he had the hypodermic dribbling to his satisfaction. 'One of several things could happen. You could break out in a rash. That's no problem. You could develop low blood pressure. That's more of a problem. Occasionally, perhaps one case in fifty thousand results in death.' He looked at Salter. 'Okay?' He moved out of Salter's vision.

'Why are you telling me this?' asked Salter.

'We have to under the law, so that you can refuse the injection if you like.'

'But then you couldn't take the X-rays.' Salter wished he could see the man at least.

'That's right.'

I have three seconds to decide, Salter thought. Exit one policeman with an infarction of the heart. The hell with it, let him stick the needle in himself. I'm going home.

'Go ahead,' he said.

The doctor shoved the needle into his arm and looked deep into his eyes. He loves me after all, Salter thought.

'All right. If anything were going to happen, it would have shown up by now,' the doctor remarked to the technician, and left.

After that it was just chilly and boring, and

twenty minutes later Salter shuffled along the corridor and got dressed.

★   ★   ★

'So what did they say?' Annie asked.

'Nothing.'

'Didn't you ask?'

'They said they'd send a report to the specialist. I have to see him again on Tuesday.'

'For God's sake find out what's going on, will you, Charlie? It's you it's happening to. You won't lose face by asking.'

★   ★   ★

The evening was spent beginning the preparations for the trip. Angus was still avoiding his father, and Seth was out collecting the money from his paper-route. Salter watched Annie fuss around, accumulating a pile of warm clothes in the middle of the living-room floor. Salter was slightly irritated at her keen encouragement of this first attempt of his to be his own son's Big Brother, and he made no attempt to help beyond pointing out that everything had to go into one bag. He took time off to

152

telephone Fred Staver, the man who had installed the screen door, to ask if he remembered where the door had been bought, and he was moderately encouraged when Staver, after hearing the problem, promised to look around himself for a wheel. Fred Staver, in their experience, could fix anything. Eventually it was bedtime, and Annie, who had refused to rise to Salter's surliness, slid naked under the duvet.

Salter tried to keep his distance. 'It's not that warm yet,' he grunted, but she scratched his belly in invitation and he gave in. A little later he looked at the bedside clock.

'Fifteen minutes, nearly,' he said.

'To what?'

'From the beginning.'

'You timing us now?'

'Just curious. Not bad, though, is it, at my age?'

'Wonderful,' she said. 'Practice makes perfect, or better, anyway.'

'What do you mean by that?'

'When we first got married you would have needed a stopwatch.'

'I was a raw, inexperienced youth then.'

'Was that it? I thought it was me. Hotter than a fire cracker. Anyway, you were twenty-eight.'

'I was a late bloomer. Now shut up. All this talk is getting me going again, and I need a little nap between rounds.'

'Poor old man.' She stroked his belly again, but just to say good-night. 'Soon be time to put the clocks back,' she murmured, fitting herself, spoon-like, into his shape.

Salter dozed, letting daylight-saving time take him into the end of fall and on into the winter. If I live that long, he thought. First, though, some fishing. He reached out and pulled Annie closer into him. Fifteen minutes wasn't bad, he told himself. Darling was probably bragging.

CHAPTER FOUR

On Monday morning Fred Staver phoned before Salter left for work. 'Appen you've found yon widget?' he asked. Staver had immigrated thirty years before from the north of England but he still spoke in a dialect so thick you could hear the batter pudding cooling on the doorstep.

'I haven't found a plastic wheel yet, Fred, no,' Salter said.

'Aye. Well, nobbut a smell of one at

Tunney's, lad, and if Tunney's havena' one, no booger 'as. But I found out t'bloke 'oo makes 'em. 'Appen you've got a bit o' pencil or summat?'

'Aye,' Salter said.

'Aye. Well, then. It's Graberg Doors out at Weston. A little factory, like.'

Weston. A factory in an industrial park on the edge of the city which would take an hour to get to and another hour to find when you got there. 'What's the street address, Fred?'

''Ere it is, then. Eight, got that, eight, that's right, eight, seven, two, one. Eight, seven, two, one—big number 'nt it? Ryle Boulevard.'

'Spell it, would you, Fred?'

'Aye. R-I-E-L—Ryle.'

'It's pronounced Ree-el, Fred. Riel was a famous rebel. They hanged him.'

'Aye, well, they named a boulevard after him, too. Ah've never been to t'place meself but 'appen you'll find it easy enough.'

'Thanks, Fred. Thanks for your trouble.'

'No trouble, mate. But listen, listen. If you do find t'place, buy a couple for me, eh? I might 'ave a need for one. No point in wasting a journey is there? Ta-ta.'

Before he went to the office, Salter called in at the Canadian Tire store and bought a

155

cheap rod and reel for Angus, some mosquito repellent, and a gallon of camp fuel. Then he moved on to Ziggy's where he picked up a dozen Mars bars and a giant can of mixed nuts. When Salter went fishing he liked to eat Mars bars and drink beer while he was waiting for a bite. In the evenings, in the cabin, he liked nuts with his beer. He never ate chocolate or nuts at any other time. He tucked the goodies into a corner of his trunk so that Annie wouldn't see them and make fun of him.

At the office, for something to do, he phoned the dealer who had sold Tanabe the prints. 'Mr MacLeod,' he asked, 'we'd like to talk to Mr Tanabe more than ever. Are you sure you have no Toronto address for him, a hotel or something he used on one of his visits?'

'No. I'll ask Hajime when he comes in, but Gene used to give me a cheque and disappear. I never knew where he stayed. Have you tried his store in Vancouver?'

'Yes, he's gone missing from there, too. If he comes back or calls, get hold of me right away will you?'

'Of course. I hope nothing has happened to him.'

'Probably not. I don't think we're dealing

with gangsters. Thanks, Mr MacLeod.'
Salter hung up.

It was time for another chat with Nelson.

*   *   *

He found the assistant at home, and once
more in a very distressed state. He let Salter
in to the living-room and stood waiting for
him to speak.

'Can I sit down?' Salter asked.

'If you want.' Nelson took the chair
farthest from Salter and continued to stare at
him.

'Something wrong?' Salter asked.

'Nothing to do with you, Inspector. Just a
lover's quarrel.'

Again. 'Hauser has been here?'

'No. He phoned. We're finished. I won't
have him checking up on me.'

Salter was out of his depth. 'What was he
checking up on you for?'

Nelson stood up and began walking round
the room, like an actor expressing agitation,
although his distress was very real. 'The same
thing you were. Where was I the night of the
fire? I told him I went home to my parents, so
he went over to see them with an excuse
about me wanting him to pick up a jacket I'd

157

left there that night. Naturally they thought there was a mistake; they told him they hadn't seen me for two weeks. So he made a scene about how I was being unfaithful to him. My parents live in Oakville! There were neighbours in for bridge! They have been extremely supportive ever since I told them about myself, but my father was very upset when he phoned. Then this morning Jake phoned, pleading with me, but I've made up my mind. He says he'll kill himself, but I'm not giving in to blackmail, either.'

'Mr Nelson, perhaps if we talked about my problem, it might help you to forget yours for a minute.'

'I'm sorry, Inspector. I'm sorry.' Nelson took a breath and returned to his chair.

Just then the telephone rang and Nelson lifted it, listened for a moment, then laid the receiver on the coffee table, where it beeped for a few moments to let him know what he had done, then was silent.

'Right,' Nelson said again, determinedly. 'Go ahead.'

'I've checked up on everyone Drecker dealt with in the last few months from the list you gave me. Nothing very unusual, except for the old Japanese gentleman who was interested in something Drecker sold. Do you remember anything more about him.'

'No more than I told you. He was in several times. He bought a box from us, a sort of cabinet about the size of an attaché case, with a fitted tray inside, with a lovely glossy finish. He asked me where it came from but I didn't know. Drecker just appeared with it one day the way he often did, and I thought it was from a garage sale. He wasn't in when I sold the box so the man came back next day. He and Drecker spent a long time in the back room, and when they came out Drecker looked a bit uptight. I remember him saying something like, "I can't tell you any more. I bought it, box and contents, from a man who walked in the shop. I get a lot of stuff off the street that way. I don't know who he was." The old man came back once more a day or so later, and Drecker wouldn't even talk to him. Told him to stop bothering him. When the old man left, Drecker told me if he ever came back I was to say Drecker was out. I didn't think anything of it at the time, except that he had probably swindled someone else.'

'It sounds to me as if the contents of the box might have been worth a few bucks.'

'Yes? As I say, I never saw what was in it. When it appeared in the store it was empty. It

159

just had a label on the side "To be held until called for". Drecker had me take that off.'

'And that was that?'

'Yes. Except that after the old man left I heard Drecker shouting at someone on the phone. I'm fairly sure that it was about the box. After he'd finished talking, though, he seemed a lot calmer as if whoever it was had satisfied him. Why, do you think there was some kind of Japanese Maltese Falcon in the box?'

'Don't be silly,' Salter said, embarrassed that Nelson was toying with the same melodramatic fancy that he had entertained. 'I think it's more likely the old man was trying to establish the—what do you call it—the provenance of the box. We know who he is. He's a dealer himself.'

'Ah. The genuine antique Japanese box turned out to be made in Taiwan. Could be. We sold it "as is", though.'

'Another question, Mr Nelson. Who had access to the store? Who had keys?'

Nelson now looked nervous. 'Drecker, of course,' he began. 'His wife, I think. She is part owner and she goes down on Sundays sometimes to look the stock over. She never comes near during normal hours.'

'Anyone else?' Salter watched with interest

as Nelson's face turned dark red.

'Yes. Me.'

'You?'

'Yes. I had keys to the doors. I worked late sometimes, and Drecker let me use the workroom to refinish things I wanted to sell.'

'Did you ever spend the night there?'

'Sometimes. There were always a couple of couches or settees to sleep on.'

'Why?' Salter looked around the elegant apartment. 'Why would you sleep there? It's not far away.'

'It was a place to go if I wanted to be alone.'

'Not with anyone?'

'No, never. To get away from someone.'

'I see. Your room-mate.'

'Yes. This isn't the first fight we've had, though I swear it will be the last.'

Salter pondered this. 'Mr Nelson,' he asked. 'Did you ever leave the keys around anywhere? Where are they now, for example?'

Again Nelson looked very agitated. 'I don't know. I lost them.'

'You lost them? When?'

'The day before the fire.'

'Christ Almighty. You don't know where, of course. In here?'

161

'No. I'm sure I didn't leave them around here. I don't remember handling them after I left the store. They are probably in the store somewhere.'

'Did you look around for them, the next day?'

'Yes, I did. I couldn't find them.'

'What did they look like? Two or three keys on a ring?'

'No. That's what I don't understand. There were four of them—both the doors had two locks—and they weighed a ton. They's why I tried to leave them in the store most of the time.'

'And if you brought them home, what did you do with them?'

'If I took them out of my pocket, I put them on the bureau in my bedroom.'

'I see. And did you? That night?'

'I don't remember. When I came home Jake was in a difficult mood and we started quarrelling right away. As I told you, it went on and on—we didn't even have any dinner. Then I got sick of it and left.'

'So you didn't change. What were you wearing?'

'My suede jacket. Oh, for God's sake, Inspector, do you think Jake stole them?'

'Maybe he thought you went back to the

store.'

'And followed me and burned the place down? He isn't a *killer*.' Nelson was shouting now.

'He did have access to the keys, though, didn't he?'

Nelson refused to answer.

'I think I'd better find him,' Salter said. 'Any ideas where he might be? We've tried all the obvious places.'

'I told you I don't know where he is.' Nelson was breaking down again.

'All right, Mr Nelson. He's probably just—' Salter nearly said 'sulking'—'hiding out somewhere. We'll find him. If he gets in touch with you, let me know, will you?' Salter let himself out of the apartment. He knew what Superintendent Orliff would say: 'A lovers' quarrel, revenge, and then flight when he realized what he'd done.' It seemed obvious. But Salter's hunch was growing stronger.

There was nothing to do until Hauser was found, or the mysterious Japanese turned up, but he needed to think, and he didn't want to be questioned by Gatenby or Orliff, especially Orliff. So he drove home, put the broken screen door in the trunk of his car and drove out to Weston to find the factory. As he expected, it took him nearly an hour to find the place, but when he finally located it he got a pleasant surprise. It was a one-man operation—a kind of carpenter's shop except that the material was aluminium. The owner-manufacturer listened carefully to Salter's problem, then looked at the door. Without a word he turned back to the workshop and led Salter to a huge box of plastic wheels. 'How many?' he asked.

Salter gaped. 'Give me six.' he said.

'Six dollars,' the man said, and dropped the wheels into Salter's hand.

'Will I be able to put them on myself?' Salter asked.

'Sure. There are two little prongs. Open the prongs with a screwdriver or something, and the broken wheel will drop out. Then you drop your new wheel in. No problem.'

'Don't I have to unscrew the corner?' The corner of the frame was held in place by a metal screw.

'Don't unscrew the corner. Don't touch the corner. Leave the corner alone. Just open the prongs and drop the wheel in.'

'Can you show me?'

'Mister, you want me to repair the door? I charge a minimum of thirty-eight dollars for service. Do it yourself. Just open the prongs.

Okay?'

'Right,' Salter said, briskly. But he knew when he came to do it there would be one other small thing the man had not mentioned as being too obvious, like, 'Put the wheel in the right way round, dull side up.' Ah shit, he thought. After I've broken three wheels I ought to know everything there is to know. He drove home and put the door back on the third floor deck, leaving the wheels on his wife's dressing-table. Later, he thought. Later.

★　　　★　　　★

Tuesday was a lost day, except that he found out early that he had some years to live. He reported to the hospital at eight o'clock and was led into an examination room and asked to take his clothes off and lie down on a piece of apparatus that supported him with his legs apart and his feet in the air. A medical aide chatted continuously about how the examination was a bit personal but not painful.

The doctor appeared, the same specalist who had looked at him the first time, nodded to Salter and went to work. Speaking from somewhere below Salter's feet, he said, 'You

165

will feel this pass over the membrane. When it does, tell me.'

Salter ignored him. Very soon he felt something sliding through his vitals on its way over the membrane. After that nothing happened for a few minutes while the doctor searched in Salter's innards. He looked up once and said to Salter, 'How old are you?'

'Forty-seven.' He's appalled by my bladder, Salter thought, which looks like that of a ninety-year-old syphilitic.

The doctor grunted, and soon thereafter an icy sliding sensation began again as the instrument was withdrawn. He lay waiting for the verdict.

'You have a slightly enlarged prostate,' the doctor said.

That's what de Gaulle died of, Salter thought.

'Not too abnormal for your age. The X-rays showed nothing, and the other tests are negative, too. I can't find anything wrong with you. Drink lots of liquids.'

'Thanks. Will I be able to work today?'

'What do you do?'

'I'm a police inspector.'

'Mainly sitting down? You will be all right. You'll want to urinate more frequently, and you may find a trace of blood in your urine.

166

Nothing to stop you working.'

'Thank you. I'm all right then?'

'As far as I'm concerned, yes.'

Of course I may have eleven other diseases that do not come under your specialty, but for you I'm fine. 'Thank you,' he said again.

The doctor left and Salter got dressed, turning his back on the aide to examine himself. He looked normal, but much smaller than he remembered.

★   ★   ★

At the office he phoned Vancouver again, but Tanabe had not turned up. Another check showed that Jake Hauser was still missing. But he had little time to brood about his collection of dead ends. Very shortly he became acutely uncomfortable and he made a dive for the washroom. When he came back to the office he prepared to start work on some kind of report for Orliff, but within ten minutes he was off to the washroom again. He stayed in the office for an hour during which time he visited the washroom six times, until he got sick of the sympathetic clucking of his sergeant. At noon he said, 'I'm going home where I can pee in peace. If anything interesting happens, call me there.

167

Tomorrow I'm going to hand over this case to Munnings and Hutter.'

He drove home and let himself into the house, looking for aid and comfort, before he remembered that Annie had a job and the house was empty. Supposing the news at the hospital had been bad, he thought. I might be lying here with three months to live and she's off looking for the props for a beer commercial. He lay on the bed, waiting for the next false call of nature, and the phone rang. It was Annie.

'What did he say?' she asked.

'Who?'

'Charlie, please. I've been waiting for you to call all day. I just called your office and they said you had gone home. What did the doctor say?'

'He said I'm all right.'

'Oh, Charlie.' Her breath poured out in a huge sigh. 'You don't sound very happy about it.'

'Well, you know how it is. You find out everything is all right, then five minutes later you are back in the world looking for something to worry about. Were *you* very worried?'

'Not until Blostein said it might be serious.'

'You talked to Blostein about me?'

'Yes. I'm sorry. I wanted to know.'

It didn't matter now. Salter decided on a joke. 'I'll tell you what,' he said. 'If I become impotent, don't discuss it with Jenny, will you?'

'Why? You still think if she played her cards right she could win you?'

He laughed. 'Hang up now,' he said. 'I've got a problem.'

'What?'

He told her.

Now it was her turn to laugh. 'Want me to come home and take your mind off it?'

'How? Oh Jesus, no. My guess is that I'll be sleeping in the spare room for about a month, trying to keep a low profile. Goodbye now, I've got to go.'

For the rest of the day Salter read, trotted, and wondered at specialists who regarded his condition as not interfering with his work. Once he made an attempt to fix the screen door, but he was unable to concentrate with the ferocity the job required, so he did no more than establish that there were no prongs visible to the naked eye; the instructions had broken down at the first step. He was not much cheered by the increase in the number of wasps on the deck. They seemed to be

169

hiving, or whatever wasps did, and there were seven or eight round him all the time. They made the deck unusable, and because the glass door had to be kept closed until the screen was fixed, the third floor of the house was ten degrees warmer than the rest. Things were shaping for a crisis.

★   ★   ★

Next morning Salter tested his condition by staying home until ten o'clock. The house was empty. He lay on the bed, letting his mind wander. What I should do, he said to himself, is to systematically review all the possibilities, eliminate the ones that don't work, and proceed from there. Right. How to start? Pretend you're talking to Gatenby. Right. Here we go, then. We have several possibilities, Sergeant. One: Drecker stole the box at the garage sale. Unlikely. Drecker from all accounts was a chiseller, not a thief. Two: Drecker bought the box at the garage sale, and Murdrick, in charge of the sale, pocketed the money and told his wife the box had disappeared. No, because if that were the case why had Drecker refused to tell Tanabe where he got it? Three: Drecker and Murdrick were in league, and Drecker then was covering for himself in case the box was hot. Possibly Murdrick had found his wife's guardianship of the box ridiculous after forty years and felt safe in stealing it. Possibly Murdrick had thought the old man would die. Now, Frank, who set fire to Drecker's store? One: Tanabe, in revenge after he had tracked the box down. Possible, if we could figure out a way the old man could have got into the basement. Two: Murdrick. The two thieves had fallen out over the price of the box. The most likely. He's shifty, mean and possibly capable of it, especially if slightly drunk. But how did *he* get in? Three: Nelson, the assistant. Possible, if Julia Costa was covering for him, although he didn't seem violent. But he loathed Drecker, he had a set of keys, and there might be some other reason not yet apparent. Four: Nelson's lover, Hauser. After the quarrel he might have chased over to the store, having stolen Nelson's keys. But if he stole Nelson's keys he would know that Nelson was not in the store. But a wanton bit of arson was still possible. Five: the mistress, Costa. Drecker might have given her a key for their assignations (nice word, that, Frank). But, like Nelson, she had an alibi, and there was no good reason that we know of. Six: the wife. Possible. She had a set of keys and a lot to gain. But she had also been in Alberta that night, Charlie. She could have hired someone, Frank. In Toronto it is possible to hire the services of a killer or an arsonist, or just a leg-breaker, but you have to be well-connected, and on these grounds Mrs Drecker seems out of it. Seven: Darling, because Drecker had swindled him. How, though?

Salter sighed. It is, of course, possible, Frank, that this is one of those nice old-fashioned mysteries, in which Nelson will turn out to be apparently gay, while all the time a practising closet heterosexual in love with Drecker's wife, and the two of them had planned it together to get the insurance and live happily ever after, doing yoga on an annuity. In that case, Nelson's lover doesn't exist, and Nelson is using him as a cover to screw around with the wife, the mistress, the lady across the hall, and even Mrs Murdrick, like in a play I saw once at Stratford (Ontario), of which all I can remember is that the hero was named Horney and all the other men thought he was impotent and trusted him with their wives. Maybe they are all in it together, and they have invented Tanabe (really a clever out-of-work male impersonator aged twenty-two with fair hair)?

Screw this, thought Salter. I'd better get back to work. He could check on at least one of the theories right away. He called the office and told Gatenby to expect him at noon. Then he drove to Queen Street, turned right along Murdrick's street and parked on the corner where he made a phone call from the telephone booth. He went back to his car and waited an hour, and eventually Murdrick emerged alone and drove off in a panel truck to estimate the non-existent job Salter had invented. Salter waited another five minutes, then knocked on the door.

'It's all right, Mrs Murdrick,' Salter said heartily. 'No problem. I forgot to check on something. Just routine. I have to establish the movements of anyone I talk to in connection with last week's incident. Can you tell where you all were on Monday night last week?'

'Sure,' she said promptly, looking relieved. 'In Montreal. I have a sister there, and since Phil didn't have a job on I asked him if we could go down for a couple of days. It was her birthday and they had a big party. We stayed overnight. Her name is Carrier. She lives at sixty Colwood Road in St Henri.'

And there were ninety-five witnesses, thought Salter. 'Thanks, Mrs Murdrick. One last thing. Is your husband around?'

'No. He just got called out to estimate a job.'

'I just wanted to ask him how long Drecker's bathroom took him. Him and Darling, I mean.'

At first there was no bite. 'He didn't work on that job,' she said. 'He's been with some Italian company doing a mall in the West End for the last six weeks. Unless it was before then, was it?'

But Salter was trying to establish something else. 'No,' he said. 'He won't be able to help me, then. Pity. He usually does work with Darling, doesn't he, when Darling needs a tiler?'

'Oh yes. He does all Raymond's work when he can. Why?'

There must be some technique, thought Salter, for finding out what you need to know without stumbling around like this. What I've done now is made sure that as soon as Murdrick comes back he will hear I've been checking up on Darling. 'It's just that I need to know who has been in Drecker's store lately. I've already talked to Mrs Darling, but I forgot to ask him who his helper was. I will.

Thanks.' Salter smiled to show that the matter was of no importance, and left. Clumsy, but he had got the connection he wanted between Murdrick and Darling.

★   ★   ★

Salter drove back down Queen Street to where his father lived. The two men had little in common any more, but Salter tried to visit whenever he was in the neighbourhood.

The old man opened the door of the upper duplex and expressed surprise, but not a lot of pleasure, at his visitor. 'Hello, stranger,' he said. 'Lost your way?'

'I was here last week, Dad,' Salter said, 'And the week before that you had dinner with us.'

He followed his father upstairs and greeted May, his father's girlfriend, who was sitting drinking coffee in the tiny living-room. She smiled at him and disappeared into the kitchen. In the five months Salter had known her she had said only about three words. She was a stout, mushroom-coloured lady with wig-like hair and a contented expression. Salter's father had taken up with her after being a widower for years when her husband, an old buddy of his, had died. The effect had been to change the old man from a misanthropic bigot, grinding slowly and sourly through his retirement, into an old lecher who never failed in Salter's company to hint at the sexual capers he and May got up to. The change was an improvement because it relieved Salter and Annie of the sole responsibility for the old man's emotional welfare, with all the attendant dutiful and difficult visits and invitations. It was true that they thought of him less often now, a fact the old man was quick to notice.

Now he said, 'What are you up to, son? Caught any drug smugglers lately?'

'I'm not on the Drug Squad, Dad.'

'That's right, I forgot. You're a dogsbody these days. What are you doing, then?'

For lack of any other topic, Salter told him something of the case. The old man listened judiciously.

'Ten to one it's the old Jap,' he said. 'Scheming lot, they are.'

When, thought Salter, have you ever spoken ten words in your life to a Japanese? To change the subject, he told his father about Annie's job.

'You want to watch that, son,' his father said immediately. 'When they start getting restless, the trouble's usually there.' He pointed with a thumb to the bedroom. Then he looked around to make sure May was out of hearing, and leaned forward confidentially. 'Itchy pants,' he explained. 'You been up to the mark lately? Keep an eye on her.'

Salter had been raised by this man in an atmosphere of Anglo-Saxon puritanism, but now late-blooming lust had released in his father a powerful strain of dirty-mindedness that Salter found difficult to cope with. This, combined with an awareness that the same idea had crossed his own mind, made him change the subject again. 'I'm taking Angus fishing next week,' he said.

'He's the oldest one, isn't he?' His father insisted on confusing the two boys in spite of having seen them at least once a month all their lives. 'Is he keen on fishing, then?'

'Not as far as I know.'

'Ah. Doesn't surprise me.'

'Why?' Salter asked, thinking: This is silly, what do I care what he thinks? But now he was irritated enough to be looking for a quarrel.

'Well, he's not very typical, is he? I mean, not really a man's boy, is he?'

'What the hell are you talking about?'

'Don't get uptight, son. I've watched that

boy. He's a bit off the mark, if you ask me. Too much of his mother's hand. What's he interested in?'

'He wants to be an actor.'

'Ah. There you are then. What did I tell you?'

'You don't have to be abnormal to be an actor, for Christ's sake.'

'Watch your language, son. May's in the kitchen. No. But a lot of them are. Fruits, I mean.'

'We caught him with some skin books last week. What do you make of that?'

'He's trying to repress it, see. But it's bound to come out. Never mind. The other one seems all right.' His father never spoke the boys' names, finding them affected, even though they had been used in Annie's family for generations.

Salter stood up. 'Worry about yourself, will you,' he said noisily. 'Let *us* worry about Angus.'

'Don't lose your temper, son. Don't forget I've had more experience than you've had. I knew a *mechanic* who was a fruit, once, believe it or not. When are you coming back?'

'You are supposed to be coming for supper next week. Annie called you.'

'That's right. I got the message. Oh, son, see if you can stop her from giving us any of her chowder muck. I don't like it, and nor does May. Make it a proper dinner, or we might as well stay at home.' A proper dinner, for Salter's father, meant meat, potatoes, peas and carrots, all with a lot of gravy, followed by something soaked in custard.

'Annie hasn't served you chowder for ten years, but I'll remind her,' Salter said, and slammed the door behind him.

That afternoon he sat down with the telephone and tried seriously to find a suspect with a flaw, or a flaw in his suspect. He began by phoning the Montreal police, asking for Sergeant Henri O'Brien who owed him a favour. O'Brien was delighted to hear from him.

'Charlie,' he shouted, 'what can I do for you? When are we going to the races again?' O'Brien had introduced Salter to harness-racing while they were cooperating on a case.

'Soon, Onree. Soon. Come to Prince Edward Island for your holidays this year and we'll go to Charlottetown races every night.'

'Sounds terrific, Charlie. I've got a cousin with a farm in St Louis. Is that nearby?'

'Not really. We stay with my wife's family near Cavendish. But I can get away. Every

179

night.'

'Ah. Sure.' There was a delicate pause. O'Brien continued. 'So what's the problem, Charlie?'

Salter explained. A routine check that the Murdricks were at a party in St Henri on the previous Monday.

'It's a pleasure,' O'Brien said. 'I'll call you back.'

Next he called Mrs Drecker. 'We are looking into the possibility that your husband may have stumbled across something valuable which someone else wanted,' he said. Like the goddam Maltese Falcon. 'Can you remember as far back as June? Did you and he, or just he alone, go to a garage sale in Woodstock?' He held the phone a foot away from his ear, waiting for her reply.

'Where's Woodstock?'

'It's about ninety miles away. On Highway Four-o-one.'

'No,' she said promptly. 'Never. Cyril wouldn't go out of town. He said it wasn't worth it. When we went picking we always did three or four sales, and in a place like Woodstock you would only have one in a day. It wasn't worth the trip, according to Cyril.'

'You're sure? Not even for something special?'

'Just a minute. What day?'

'The fourteenth.'

'Hold on. I'll look up my book. Whenever Cyril wanted me along I put it in my engagement book. It was usually on a Saturday; then, if I had a free day I could plan a little outing on my own. Hold on.' She put the phone down, and Salter could hear her walking along the hall. When she returned, she said, 'On June fourteen we went to three sales in the morning and two in the afternoon. All in Toronto. Got quite a bit of stuff, too.'

'Thanks.'

'Oh, Inspector. When do you think this will be cleared up? I'd like to get going again, now the funeral's over.'

'What do you mean?'

'I've been thinking. I might take the store over myself. I enjoy the trade, and all I'd need is someone to run the shop.'

'You might try that assistant, Nelson,' Salter said. Your fellow conspirator in one of my fancier theories.

'I was thinking of him. When would I be able to open up, do you think?'

'That depends on the insurance people, Mrs Drecker. When they are satisfied, you'll get your money.' Unless I catch you doing

181

headstands with Nelson.

'I'll give them a ring. Any luck yet?' She sounded about as concerned as someone inquiring after a lost wallet, Salter thought.

'Nothing firm, Mrs Drecker. We have a number of leads. I'll let you know.'

Next he called the assistant, Nelson. He described Murdrick to him and asked him if he had seen anyone like him around the store or heard his name.

'No, never,' the assistant said, after a moment. 'Never heard of him, and I don't remember seeing him. But we do get a lot of casual trade. He might have been in.'

'Thanks. No news of Hauser?'

'I was going to ask you that.'

'We're looking, Mr Nelson. We'll let you know.'

The telephone rang. It was O'Brien, from Montreal.

'Already, Onree? I only spoke to you ten minutes ago. I know. There's no such street as Colwood in St Henri, and there's no one named Carrier in the Montreal phone book. So I have a suspect with a phoney alibi and the case is closed. Something nice like that, is it, Onree?'

'No such luck, Charlie. We didn't have to check. One of the men here is related to this

Carrier. He was at the party, and he remembers the Murdricks. Worse yet, Charlie. There is a picture of the happy feast someone took that night. My man had a copy, and I'm looking at it now. He says Murdrick is right in the middle. Sorry.'

'Thanks, anyway, Onree. I'll see you in Charlottetown.'

'Look at it this way, Charlie. It is sometimes nearly as helpful if you know which horse *can't* win a race as to know who the winner will be. It helps with the triactor, anyway.'

'Right now, Onree, I've got eight horses and they've all broken stride.'

'Then you'll have to start again. That's what they do at Greenwood.'

'We're beating this metaphor or whatever it is to death. I'll talk to you later.'

'There's a call for you on the other line when you've finished with Interpol,' Gatenby said. 'That art dealer in Yorkville.'

Salter pressed a button. 'Mr MacLeod? Salter here.'

'We've found an address for Mr Tanabe,' MacLeod said, without preamble. 'Gene forgot his briefcase here one day, and he was so concerned about it I sent Hajime over in a cab. He just reminded me. Here it is.' He

183

gave an address in Fortress Hill, a district of upper-class homes in mid-town Toronto, and a name to go with it, Jacob Harz.

Salter looked up the name and dialled. 'Mr Harz? Inspector Salter here, Metro Police. I am inquiring into the whereabouts of a Mr Gene Tanabe and I am informed that he visited you recently. Do you have any idea where Mr Tanabe is now?'

There was a long pause, followed by a theatrical sigh. 'I'm afraid not, Inspector.' An old man; a comfortable, easy voice with a slight accent.

'You know Mr Tanabe?'

'Sure I know Gene.' The voice sounded surprised. 'But you want to talk to him, right?'

'I want to find him.'

There was another long silence. 'I don't know about that. Look, Inspector, can you come by the house? Not now. Tonight. I'm upstairs right now and my daughter won't let me on the stairs unless someone is with me, and the housekeeper's out for a little while. Can you do that? After work. I'll tell you a story.'

'I'm investigating a serious case, Mr Harz. Can you tell me over the phone? Now?'

'This story goes back forty years,

Inspector. Can a few hours make any difference?'

'Right. I'll be there at seven.'

'Sure. Any time. I'll tell you a story about Gene Tanabe. I figured I'd be hearing from you, one way or the other. See you tonight, then. Take care.' The old man hung up.

Gatenby put his head round the door. 'Your wife called,' he said. 'She said she's going to be working late. Can you take the boys out for a hamburger.'

Salter dialled his wife's number. 'Gatenby told me you're working late.'

'That's right, I told you I might be. We have a location shot in Markham Village. I have to get a car into the courtyard of a restaurant for a shot of beautiful people dining out. It has to be a night shot.'

'Do the beautiful people drive their cars right into restaurants, now?'

'In the ad they do.'

'What time will you be home?'

'I don't know for sure. You can come and watch if you like.' Annie named the restaurant.

'I'd look like a real horse's arse, wouldn't I, hanging about keeping tabs on you.'

'Is that what you would be doing, Charlie? You don't have to.'

'Ten o'clock?' Salter asked. 'Eleven?'

'I don't *know*, Charlie. We may have a drink afterwards. Can you take the boys to McDonald's?'

'I hate McDonald's,' Salter said, who had never set foot in it. 'I'll feed them something.'

'I'll tell you if the plans change. Things happen quickly around here.'

'Don't call after eight. I won't be there.'

'Why not?'

'I'll be working,' Salter said. 'I have to see a guy in Forest Hill.'

'See you in bed, then. 'Bye, Charlie.'

It was three o'clock. Salter sat with his head in his hands and stared at the wall. Tonight, he thought, I will hear a story about how an old Japanese art dealer finally found some pictures he thought he had lost. It will be an interesting story but it will have nothing to do with the case because on the night of the fire the old Japanese will be able to show that he was in Tokyo, visiting relatives. Too many people had testified that Gene Tanabe was not the kind of man to go around burning down buildings for Salter to have much hope. On the other hand he didn't have anything better to do.

'Tea?' Gatenby asked.

Salter looked through his sergeant. 'What haven't I done?' he asked himself.

'I don't know, do I?' There was a note of reproach in Gatenby's voice. 'You haven't told me all of it yet.'

'Sorry. I thought you were picking it up as we went along. You want to go over it? I'll tell you the whole story and you can tell me what I haven't thought of.'

'Like Holmes and Watson!' Gatenby cried. 'But I get to be Holmes, right? Okay, go ahead. Let me pour the tea first.'

'Shut the door if you are going to horse around. I don't want Orliff listening.'

'Right. Go ahead, my dear Watson.'

Salter began with the fire. He outlined all the facts and then concluded, 'So it seems likely that someone set the fire and then let himself out the front door. So somebody had a key and the obvious one is Nelson. Failing him, his boyfriend, Hauser.' Carefully, as he had done for two days, Salter tried to remain objective and let the evidence accumulate, but nothing he could do would prevent his hunch from growing more and more into a certainty.

'But Nelson's got a good alibi.'

'Yes, and anyway, I don't get any smell off him. But he took the keys home and that is

187

the last time he remembers having them. It seems obvious, then, that Hauser picked up the keys after Nelson left, drove over to the store where he thought Nelson was spending the night, and set fire to it.'

'But if Nelson left the keys behind, then Hauser knew he wasn't in the store.'

'Right. So Hauser didn't do it. Good.'

There was a silence for a while.

'Well, that's the end of that one,' Gatenby said. 'Any other possibilities? Suppose Nelson didn't leave the keys behind?'

'Then Hauser is more likely to have gone to the store, right?'

'I was thinking more of where Nelson *did* leave the keys.'

'They weren't in the store. We checked.'

'So he still had them on him when he got to Julia Costa's apartment. Unless he dropped them somewhere.'

'Well, Costa didn't do it because Nelson was with her the rest of the night. We'd better not get too buried in this. Nelson could have just lost the keys, and anyway, someone else, someone we don't know about, could have picked the lock. The door wasn't barred.'

'Could anyone else have had a key?'

After a while Salter said, 'Julia Costa. But

188

we've ruled her out already.'

'If we keep ruling everybody out, we won't get anywhere. Maybe this Costa woman did it with Nelson—they've given each other an alibi, haven't they.'

Salter shook his head. 'Nelson wasn't lying. The woman across the hall heard the row, and he did go straight over to Costa's. But you've given me an idea. I don't know if Julia Costa had a key. If she did, maybe others did, too. Nelson said that Drecker often had more than one woman. We may have to look right outside this gang. But let's find out first if Costa did have a key. Come on, let's go and see her now.'

'Me, too?'

'Sure. Stay quiet and watch. Put your new raincoat on. With that hair of yours they'll think you're the Deputy Chief checking up on *me*. I'll just say you're a colleague.'

'Okay, Charlie. I'll just get a match to chew on and we'll be all set.'

★   ★   ★

They found Julia Costa alone in the store arranging a collection of Mexican furniture made of straw and leather and grey wood. Salter introduced his sergeant as 'Mr

189

Gatenby', and the sergeant sat on the arm of a chair to watch his man at work. Salter explained about the possibility of an extra key and Julia Costa stopped him before he could put the question.

'I have a key, Inspector,' she said. 'It's in my purse. Two, actually, one for each lock. You want me to get them?'

Salter looked at Gatenby who nodded solemnly back to Salter who then nodded to Costa. She disappeared into the back room and reappeared holding a ring with two large brass keys.

Salter took them from her. 'What were your arrangements with Drecker?' Salter asked.

'Usually he was waiting for me,' she said. She jerked a thumb at Gatenby. 'Does he know the whole story?'

Gatenby looked away as Salter nodded.

'Yes. Well, then. We would arrange to meet in the flat in the evening after dinner. If he got held up I could let myself in and wait for him.'

'Did anyone know you had these keys? Nelson, for instance?'

She shook her head. 'Dennis knew I slept with Drecker, but we never talked about it. It wouldn't have been—tasteful?'

190

'Good. Now I have a delicate question for you, Miss Costa. Is it possible that someone else, someone like you, could also have had a key?'

'One of his other women? You don't have to be too delicate, Inspector. I know what Cyril was like. No. For the last couple of months I've been seeing a lot more of him and I'm pretty sure there was no other woman. In fact, I know there wasn't. He said so, and the way we were, he didn't need to lie.'

'But in the past he might have given someone a set of keys and never got them back, mightn't he?'

'No. Maybe, but—no. He would get them back, I'm sure.'

Just then the door opened behind Salter, and Julia Costa's face went still. Salter looked around as Raymond Darling came in.

'Hello, hello, hello,' Darling said noisily. 'The fuzz is back, with reinforcements. What's the problem now, Inspector?'

There had been time for Salter to gather his wits and interpret the panic on Julia Costa's face as a fear that Salter would let slip her connection with Drecker.

'Just checking again, Mr Darling. We're trying to locate all possible acquaintances of the dead man. Miss Costa told us before that she knew him slightly through the trade, and I wondered if she could tell us of anyone else who might know him.'

'That's how I met him,' Darling agreed. 'Julia put me on to him when I got interested in antiques. And I did his bathroom, as I told you.'

Out of the corner of his eye, Salter could see Gatenby staring at his inspector in surprise, a sergeant again. Salter fixed him with a stony glare and turned back to listen to Darling, who was still speaking.

'I don't know why you're pestering Julia,' he said. 'I hear the queer's boyfriend has disappeared. Looks pretty obvious, doesn't it? By the way, I thought you were supposed to warn people of their rights before you questioned them?'

Salter said, 'We can talk to anyone we like in the course of an investigation, Mr Darling. If we suspect them, we warn them; then we can use what they say in evidence against them, see?'

'You've been watching too much television,' Gatenby said, trying to get back into his role.

Darling began to look angry.

'Maybe you can help us, sir,' Salter said

quickly. 'From what you knew of Drecker, would he be likely to give anyone a set of keys for the store?'

Darling reacted immediately. 'Never,' he said. 'Never. He was too cute for that. No, that assistant had the only keys.'

The accusation hung in the air.

'Oh, don't be so stupid, Raymond. Dennis wouldn't hurt a fly,' Julia Costa said.

'How do you know? Maybe Drecker made a pass at him? You don't know what Drecker was like. What the hell was that apartment of his all about?'

Salter looked at his notes, Julia Costa rummaged in her purse and Gatenby stared with an open mouth from one to the other.

Salter broke the hush. 'That's it, then, I think?' he asked inquiringly of Gatenby, who nodded firmly and stood up. The two policemen paired themselves near the door.

'If any other names occur to you, Miss Costa, or you, too, Mr Darling, call me at the station, will you?' Salter asked.

'What the hell was that all about?' Gatenby asked when they were in the car. 'Who was he?'

'Raymond Darling. Her boyfriend. Her *real* boyfriend. He doesn't know that she screwed Drecker. He wouldn't like that. Not so easy-come, easy-go as Drecker, but otherwise the same type, I would think. You remember, he's the stud who times himself.'

'My, my. Reminds me of you a bit,' Gatenby said. 'Oh, not the *looks*,' he added quickly, as Salter reacted. 'He's got your build and he walks like you. If you ever disguised yourself as a swinger, that's what you'd look like.'

'Thanks. Remind me to request a transfer to the uniformed branch tomorrow.'

★   ★   ★

'What are you going to do now, Charlie?' Gatenby asked when they were back at the station.

'I don't know yet. I'd better get something written to show Orliff before I go see this guy in Forest Hill. Then I'll see.'

He assembled the story in something like orderly fashion and began to write. When he came to Drecker's involvement, he stuck. There was a firm possibility that the Japanese box was at the bottom of all this; on the other hand, he still had not found Hauser, another firm possibility; the third firm possibility was a person or persons unknown. At this stage the report required that he give full and accurate details of all the possibilities. He dialled the pawn squad.

'The box that Cyril Drecker registered with you on—' he gave the date—'did he sell it eventually? If so, do you know the date and who to?'

'No. After the full fifteen days he could do what he liked.'

'That means that no one reported the box stolen, right?'

'Right. Not in Metro, anyway. It might have been pinched in Timbuctoo, but we don't use Interpol for stuff like this. One of these days everything will be on computer, they tell me, and we'll just be able to punch up a record of everything that's happened, everywhere in the world, but right now we limit ourselves to Toronto.' The sergeant's voice was breezy and jokey.

'So the box appeared in Drecker's store; he covered himself by listing it with you as sold to him by an anonymous stranger, then waited fifteen days, and that's the end of your interest. Right?'

'Not anonymous, Inspector. There is a name listed, but if the box was hot, the name will be phoney.' He told Salter the name.

The inspector felt an excitement like that of a winner at a race-track. 'Say that again,' he asked, unnecessarily, and heard the sergeant repeat it. 'Thanks,' he said. 'Thanks.'

'As to our interest,' the jokey sergeant continued, 'it tends to fade long before that. It usually lasts about as long as it takes me to write the name in the book.' He chuckled merrily.

'I think you are confusing "disinterested" with "uninterested", Sergeant. You've been out of the courtroom too long. 'Bye.'

Salter put the phone down, pleased with his erudition and thrilled with his discovery. 'We've got him, Frank,' he said. 'We've got him, we've got him, we've got him. Now what's that thing that O.P.P. guy is always saying at conferences—"Softlee, softlee, catchee monkey,"—that's me now, Charlee the monkee-catcher.' He pulled his papers together.

'You going to tell me, Charlie?'

'Nope.' Salter rubbed his hands together. 'No, Frank, I might spoil it if I say it out loud. You'll be the first to know, though. Now. Let's put it all together.' Salter began to write; after half an hour he came to the details of the fire and checked once more with the Fire Marshal. 'Tell me again, Mr Hayes,' he said, 'why the fire must have been started

196

from the inside.'

The investigator went over the details patiently. 'Most of all,' he concluded, 'there was no trail.'

'Trail?'

'Fuse. You'd expect to find some kind of fuse in a job like this, so that the guy igniting the fire would be safe. That place was a hell of a mess but we didn't find any evidence of a fuse. He just poured it out and set fire to it. And he must have been in the room because he only had a few seconds before the mixture would be too dangerous to be near.'

'So someone poured this stuff around, lit it, and got right out.'

'That's about the size of it.'

'You think he might have been trying to make it look accidental, like a spill?'

'I don't know. Why wouldn't he leave the can behind, then? You found it in the lane, didn't you?' A yearning for Munnings or Hutter surfaced in the Fire Marshal's voice.

But Salter didn't mind now. 'Yes,' he said. 'The Forensic lab confirms the can contained camp fuel, which is right for the job, and there were no prints on it, which means the guy was being very careful. He didn't have to be an outdoors type, did he? A lot of people use this stuff for all kinds of things, don't they?' Salter's voice was slightly pleading. He had the solution to this case, so long as there were no difficulties he hadn't seen.

'That's right. Even plumbers use it, or they used to. I use it myself in a torch I keep for odd jobs.'

'A blow-torch?' Now Salter was getting a bonus prize to go with the jackpot. 'The kind with the little pump?'

'Right. You know the kind?'

'I've seen pictures, Mr Hayes. Thanks.' Salter put the phone down carefully in case it caught fire and melted what he had just heard.

Careful now, Charlie. Make sure of every possibility. Stay cool.

It was very hard to do. Salter wrote steadily all afternoon.

CHAPTER FIVE

'Your mother's working late,' he said to the boys when he got home. 'So we're going out to eat.'

'Can we go to McDonald's?' Seth asked immediately.

'No. I'm going to take us to the best

hamburgers in Toronto.'

'Where is that?'

'A place called Hart's.'

'McDonald's is pretty good,' Seth, the arch-conservative, offered.

'Hart's is better. C'mon.'

'It won't have blue cheese and stuff on it, will it?'

He sounds like my father, Salter thought. 'No,' he said.

Angus joined in. 'C'mon, Seth. Dad has a special place. I want to see it. We can go to McDonald's any time.' Lately, between silences, Angus had been Charlie's staunchest ally in the house, hoping, Salter thought, to begin a new life.

They drove down Yonge Street past two McDonald's which Seth pointed out wistfully, and turned on to Church Street. As they were approaching Gerrard Street, the traffic obliged them to stop, and Seth pointed excitedly through the window. 'Could we go there, Dad? It looks real neat.'

Across the street was a restaurant that had been converted from a gas station, and it used the old station as its motif. The only time Salter had been in the place he had been taken there by a young girl, a student from whom he had been seeking information. For a short time Salter had experienced the classic middle-age intrigue with youth to the extent of letting the girl buy him a record of some country music that was playing at the restaurant. Taking the record home, and pretending to have bought it himself, had precipitated a giant row when Annie produced the identical record, one of a number owned by Angus that Salter regularly complained about. It had taken Annie two seconds to guess that her husband was under a small spell, and although the end result had been better relationships all round, the incident brought back several different emotions—nostalgia, guilt, and nervousness among them. Now, blocked by traffic, he swung across the road to the restaurant's parking lot.

Inside, the music of the age thumped and twanged. Around the walls, chromium-plated hub-caps and fenders hung like sculptures.

'Terrific,' Seth said, and picked up the menu.

Salter ordered a beer and two Cokes while they were making up their minds.

'I want an "Eighteen-wheeler",' Seth said.

'I think I'll have a "Tail-pipe",' Angus decided. 'What about you Dad?'

'I don't know. I can't make up my mind between an "Oil-change" and a "Gear-box". No. I'll have an "Eighteen-wheeler", too.'

When the waitress came over, Salter ordered two hamburgers and a hot-dog.

'Why didn't you tell her the proper names, Dad?' Seth asked, disappointed.

'Because I'd feel silly.'

The two boys looked at him in sympathy. Poor self-conscius old man, their faces said. It must be rotten to be like that.

Salter drove them back, conscious of having given Seth, at least, a big night out. He made sure that they had what they needed to get them through the evening and into bed, and set off for Forest Hill on foot.

The rich are different from us, thought Salter; they live in Forest Hill. Not all of them, because there are several quarters in Toronto where prices are out of the reach of all but the successful dentist class, but Forest Hill is more than a row of gaudy châteaux like Old Post Road; nor are the houses being discreetly converted into flats as in Rosedale, the original High Anglican quarter.

The village stands at the top of Spadina Road which has been one of the great caravan routes of upwardly mobile immigrants since the nineteenth century. At the bottom end of

Spadina Avenue, near the lake, the garment trade still flourishes. The best delicatessens are still here, and the Kensington Market is still called the Old Jewish Market by a previous generation, although the produce is now mostly Portuguese and West Indian. As Spadina Avenue crosses Bloor Street, it becomes Spadina Road and passes through an area inhabited mainly by respectable transients—students, 'singles' setting up house for the first time—then it climbs north through a middle-class district until it crosses St Clair Avenue and becomes for a mile or two the main street of Forest Hill Village. The village is synonymous in Toronto minds with the Jewish Establishment, although it was originally created by successful Anglos and still honours Protestant thrift in the shape of Timothy Eaton United Church, a cathedral blessed by the money of the successful shopkeeper to whom the church is dedicated, and it still contains Upper Canada College where the Canadian Establishment (including Salter, because it was a tradition in Annie's family) sends its sons.

Salter lived slightly to the east of Forest Hill and he figured it would be no more than a fifteen-minute walk to the Harz residence. He walked south to Upper Canada College, then west into a network of quiet, tree-lined streets, with large, thick-walled houses and hardly any pedestrians. As the noise from the traffic on Oriole Parkway faded, Salter took the time to enjoy the quiet lushness of the area. Autumn was at its peak, and there were leaves everywhere, enough on the trees to canopy the sidewalks, and still piled in brown and gold heaps along the sides of the road. The grass was green again after its battle with the summer sun, and the gardens still had enough bloom to make a worthy climax to the season. Some of the houses were surrounded by simple lawns, usually set with two or three trees, or clumps of white and yellow birches like the one outside Salter's bedroom window. Others tried for more elaborate effects; one house was enclosed on two sides with a superb if slightly incongruous English rose-garden. Annie was a good gardener, and the Salters had spent a lot of summer evenings, when the children were small, walking these streets, while Annie worked out what she wanted to do with their own patch of yard behind the house.

The houses were becoming bigger and the grounds larger. The address Salter was looking for turned out to be an immense house surrounded by a high fence which was itself set farther back from the street than Salter's front yard. He walked across the grass and pressed a button beside the gate, setting off a bell somewhere inside the house. The gate unlatched itself with a clicking noise, and he walked through. Now he got another surprise. Between him and the front door, a space of about two hundred feet, lay what even to Salter's eye was a very carefully made Japanese garden. There were rocks, a tiny stream, a variety of shrubs and small trees and a couple of large stones all woven into an elaborate three-dimensional tapestry that forced his eye to work in order to try to take it in. To someone used to roses and coloured borders, it looked strange, deserted and slightly arid. Salter looked at it for a long time, feeling the human hand in its composition, but unable to see the design.

'Nice, isn't it?' a voice said from the door of the house. An old man was standing in the doorway watching him. 'Come in and sit down,' he said.

Salter walked through the garden still unable to take his eye off it, until he was shaking hands with his host.

'Gene built that,' the old man said. 'That's how he paid his rent. I'm Jacob Harz. Come in, come on in.' He led the way slowly into the house, where a woman of about fifty was sitting in a straight chair.

'Good evening, Inspector,' she said.

'My daughter, Esther,' Harz said.

Salter shook hands. He looked around and picked up a quick impression of a lot of old European furniture, thick rugs, and more pictures than he was used to, most of them individually lit.

'A cup of coffee?' Esther asked.

'A cup of coffee would be nice, yes,' Salter said, feeling as if he was in a drawing-room play set in Vienna in 1910. He waited for the next line. Harz waited, too, until his daughter returned with the coffee. He had a narrow dark face and a mass of curly white hair. His hands looked as if every bone had been broken and badly set—arthritis, Salter guessed. He was wearing a dark blue woollen sports shirt, buttoned to the throat, the bottom half of a grey track suit, and carpet slippers.

Esther returned and they all sipped their coffee. Harz settled in his chair and spoke first. 'Now,' he said. 'Gene Tanabe. You're looking for him. Right? He hasn't done anything, you know.'

Salter said nothing. He was concentrating on being a policeman, on not being charmed by these people.

'But you'd like to talk to him—what do you call it?—you want him to help you in your inquiries. Right?' The old man smiled.

Salter got out his notebook. 'That's right. I'm investigating a case of arson. Mr Tanabe had some dealings with the owner of the store that burned down. I'm talking to everyone who can, or might be able to, help me. That's all. Do you know where I can find him?'

Harz sipped his coffee. 'I can tell him you're looking for him,' he offered.

'How will you do that?' Salter felt himself falling into the old man's style.

'He gets in touch with me regularly. Every day. I'll tell him.'

'I see. Good. When might that be?'

'Tonight. Tonight, Esther?' Harz looked at his daughter to confirm his reply.

'He gets in touch every day,' she said.

'Should I wait?'

Harz shook his head 'No. I'll make him get in touch with you. He's a bit frightened.'

'What of?'

'That's a thing you should ask him yourself, Inspector, when you see him.'

'All right. Would you tell him it is an official inquiry? If he doesn't present himself to us he'll be committing an offence.' Salter

206

got up, not so much to leave, but to assert that this was *his* interview, not Jacob Harz's.

'No need. Please sit down, Inspector. I said I'll tell you a story. Would you like to hear how I knew Gene?'

'If it helps.'

'It might. Sit down.'

Salter sat down again. In the presence of this old man he felt about thirteen years old.

'During the war,' Harz began, 'they took Gene's house away and put him in a concentration camp.'

'Who did?'

'You people. The Canadian government. The police. Gene spent a year in a camp.'

'I don't think they could have been concentration camps, Mr Harz. Not in Canada.'

'Sorry. The word slipped out. I just missed one myself in Germany. What did you call them over here?'

'Internment camps. But go ahead. It was wartime. There was a spy scare on.'

'Sure. I know. With us they just didn't want us to live any more. Anyway, after a year in a camp, Gene got permission to live outside, so long as he didn't go near the west coast. If he stayed away from Vancouver he could live, so he came to Toronto. Just in

207

time. Did you know they passed an ordinance in this city saying only seven hundred Japanese would be allowed to live in Toronto? City council did that. Where was I? Oh yes. I had a little antique business then, the same one Esther's got now, but I did some furniture restoring too. After the war I got back into the art business and did well—' he waved a hand at the house and garden— 'but during the war I was just getting by. I was happy to be alive, though, in a free country. Well, Gene came to me for work. I had no work and he wasn't allowed to work except as a domestic, but no one else would have him and he came back and so I let him help me out. I paid him fifty cents an hour, all I could afford and not so bad in those days. He worked like a slave. Some weeks, though, I just didn't have the work, and I couldn't pay him the full twenty dollars. But I couldn't lay him off, could I? So we made an accommodation. He moved in with us— officially he was a domestic, anyway—we had a little room, so if I couldn't pay him he wouldn't go hungry. Esther, there, thought he was her uncle, didn't you, pet?'

His daughter spoke now for the first time. 'Inspector, we're worried about him. He's too old to wander about on his own.'

'You say he was staying here, in this house?' Salter pressed.

'He always stays here,' Harz said. 'I look forward to it every year. He's family to us. He's my friend.'

Salter waited for a minute, then asked, 'When did he leave?'

'Two days after the fire. The day your sergeant talked to my daughter. She told Gene your sergeant had been in the store and he got very upset and left that night. He told me not to worry, he would keep in touch. And he has. I know how he feels. Once upon a time if I saw a policeman coming to the front door I went out the back, quick.'

'Mr Harz. If you are any judge, Mr Tanabe is running away from nothing. But he might be able to help me. Will you tell him that? And will you tell him that unless he comes forward on his own we will charge him with obstructing the police when we do find him. Which we will. Now, did he tell you why he was in Drecker's store? I have heard that he thought Drecker had some things that belonged to him.'

'Inspector, ask him yourself when you see him. I would get it all wrong. It was something about a friend who betrayed him and I didn't want to know because it made

Gene upset, all right? I don't want to know about things like that about people. I've had enough of it.'

'All right, Mr Harz.' Salter again prepared to leave, but the old man put his hand up in a gesture to stop him.

'I didn't tell you about the garden,' he said. 'After the war, Gene went back to Vancouver and started his own business. He comes to stay with us once a year on his buying trips—did I tell you that already?—and one year when he came I had been doing well and we moved in here. He said he wanted to give us a house gift, for what we did for him during the war, and he asked us if we would let him plan the garden. I said, sure. Look at it. He designed it himself and we had a landscape company working here for a month. I've had twenty years of pleasure from that garden. Each time I look at it, it seems a little bit different, or I see something new. It's peaceful.' The old man fell silent, and Salter left.

★　　★　　★

Now the streets were completely deserted, and Salter walked north, heading for Eglinton Avenue. A yellow patrol car drew

210

up alongside, then pulled away and turned right at the next corner. On an impulse, Salter turned right after the car and almost immediately it appeared behind him and the driver called to Salter to come over to the car.

'You live in the district?' the constable asked.

They are just doing their job, Salter told himself, and showed his identification.

'Right, sir, sorry. We had a couple of calls this evening about a stranger wandering round looking at the houses.'

'That was me. I was looking for a number of a friend's house.'

The constable saluted and the car pulled away.

How do yellow cars make old Jews feel, or old Japanese, he wondered. Secure? Nervous? Anyway, not nostalgic.

*   *   *

At the house Annie was not yet home and Seth was in bed. Angus was watching television and offered to make Salter some tea.

'No, thanks, Angus. Did your mother call?'

'Not while I've been home.'

Salter picked up the paper, but after a while he became aware that Angus was still around. I wish we had something to talk about, Salter thought. Maybe when he's twenty we can start again.

But Angus had something to say. He cleared his throat several times for Salter to look up, then broached his topic. 'Can I ask you something, Dad?'

'About life, yes. About my life, no,' Salter said, guessing that this was heart-to-heart.

'We never talked about those skin books I had. You know what I was reading them for?'

''The crossword?'

'No,' Angus said, breaking into giggles and trying to stay serious at the same time. 'I thought I might be gay.'

Salter stared at him. 'You *what!*'

'I thought I might be gay. You know—queer. The way some of the guys talked, I felt kind of left out.' He was still laughing in spurts at his father's joke.

'And?'

'I'm not. I'm not queer.' Angus made a face and left the room.

Annie came in at that point and Salter was too amazed at what he had heard to greet her. He told her what Angus had said and asked her what it meant.

'Just what you think it means, Charlie. Now you'll *have* to have a talk with him.'

'You know, at his age I was still throwing snowballs at little Mabel Tucker, hoping she'd notice and throw one back at me.'

'Oh, I know that,' Annie said.

'How? How do you know that?'

'Oh, Charlie. We've been married for eighteen years. It's one of the things you know about people. Let's go to bed. I'm exhausted.'

Salter's last thought as he looked at the little plastic wheels on his wife's dressing-table was to wonder if people in Forest Hill had as much trouble with screen doors as he did.

$$\star \qquad \star \qquad \star$$

'Okay, Charlie. I admit it sounds good. Darling picked up the box from Murdrick at the sale and sold it to Drecker. Drecker swindled Darling, or Darling *thinks* he did, and Darling got hold of the keys and set fire to the store. You figure Darling got the keys while he was working on Drecker's bathroom; maybe Drecker let him have a set so he could work when the store was closed. You also think Darling could have another

213

motive—if he'd found out about Drecker and his girlfriend. So what about Darling's alibi?'

Orliff was leading Salter through his report.

'I'll break it,' Salter said.

'So go and ask Darling why Drecker listed the box as being sold by him.'

'No. I don't want to move until I can hit Darling with everything. I want to drown him. Right now he thinks he's totally in the clear. If I can hit him with a packet all at once, he'll break down. The alibi is phoney. He cooked it up with his wife.'

Orliff loked back through his notes. 'Did Darling's wife seem to be lying when she spoke to you?'

'No,' Salter admitted. 'But it's a phoney alibi, I know it.'

'Interesting,' Orliff said. 'This box. It sounds like an old movie I saw on television the other night. You know the one? With Humphrey Bogart?'

Salter shook his head. 'No,' he said thinking: Christ Almighty.

'Had that fat guy, Sidney Greenstreet, in it.'

'No.'

'And that sinister little guy, Peter Lorre. What was it called?'

'I don't know. I've never seen it,' Salter said doggedly.

'I'll remember in a minute. Probably all bullshit, though.' Orliff paused and looked over Salter's report. 'There's one thing I don't like about all this, Charlie. You don't like Darling, do you?'

'No, I don't. What's that got to do with it?'

'Don't get tunnel vision, that's what. Darling is a suspect, right. So is this pansy, Hauser. When you find him don't be surprised if he's still covered in soot. And the old Japanese, too. Keep your options open. Investigate the case, all of it. Look, some of the heat is off the Homicide Squad now— they've found that rapist. We could give it back to them—the whole case—in pretty good shape. Why don't I do that?'

'Oh no, for Christ's sake!' Salter saw his chance slipping away. 'It's *my* case. If I can nail Darling it will do me some good.'

'That's right, it would. But don't make a goddamn fool of yourself, okay? Take a couple more days, go see Tanabe, but keep an open mind, do you hear?'

Salter said nothing. Orliff was right and he was offering protective advice, not threats. But Salter was certain of himself and eager to get on with it. Two days would have to be enough.

'All right,' Orliff said. 'Keep me in touch.' He nodded to dismiss Salter and clipped the report to the neat stack he was accumulating on the case, after making the inevitable little note that Salter couldn't see.

When Salter got back to his office, Gatenby was waiting for him in a state of excitement. 'An anonymous call, Charlie,' he said. 'Someone saw a silver Jeep drive away from the scene just before the fire started. And they've found Hauser. He's in Toronto General in bad shape. He got beaten up last night. And someone called Harz phoned, very urgent.'

Salter looked at the sergeant for a moment, then smiled.

'Okay. Put a guard on Hauser. What's Harz's number again?'

Gatenby gave it to him and Salter dialled.

'He's coming here, tomorrow,' Jacob Harz said. 'You want to come over? He's a little bit afraid, so take it easy, will you?'

Like all policemen, Salter had had his share of being regarded as the Establishment thug, but it hurt to hear Jacob Harz slip into the assumption, and, in his slightly edgy condition, he reacted badly. He said, 'I had planned to bring my sergeant over, Mr Harz.

216

He likes interrogating people, especially if they don't confess too quickly. He's lost a couple of cases, though, before we got what we wanted. You got a basement we can use, and a chair? I'll bring the matches.'

On the other side of the room Gatenby had paused in his tea-making activities. His glasses had slipped to the end of his nose and his mouth hung open as he stared at Salter.

'Please, Inspector,' the old man said. 'No jokes. These things happen.'

'So do arson, murder, rape, and beating children to death. Every day. I'll be over late this afternoon.' He hung up the phone. 'Frank,' he said, 'have you ever in your entire career hit anyone?'

'Only once.' Gatenby smiled at the memory. 'I was trying to separate a couple of winos, old chaps they were, who were fighting in that little park at Church and Queen. They were making a lot of noise and it was late, but they were too far gone to hurt each other. Hysterical they were, really. I tried to talk them down but they couldn't hear me, so I gave each of them a little slap round the face. It did the trick. They both started to cry and I made them shake hands.'

Headline, thought Salter: METRO POLICEMAN BRUTALLY ASSAULTS

DERELICTS. POLICE COMMISSION PROMISES FULL INQUIRY. CONSTABLE GATENBY SUSPENDED. 'Then what?' he asked.

'I left them alone. The last I saw of them they were sitting on the bench, crying their eyes out. When I came back, about half an hour later, they were gone. I could have been reported if anyone was watching, but I didn't *hurt* them.'

POLICEMAN ABANDONS WOUNDED PRISONERS. CITIZENS' COMMITTEE DEMANDS SUSPENSION.

'I'm going to talk to these people, Frank. I probably won't be back today, but I'll call in.'

'Watch out for the old man, boss. Make sure he doesn't try any Tae Kwon Do on you.'

'He's nearly eighty, Frank.'

'They keep themselves in shape, those people. Eat a lot of raw fish.' Gatenby chuckled away to himself at his own wit.

★ ★ ★

First, Salter drove over to Washington Avenue, and found, as he was half afraid he would, a silver Jeep parked in the street outside Nelson's apartment. Nelson let him

218

in silently and Salter came to the point quickly.

'Mr Nelson, on the night of the fire, you took a cab to Julia Costa's apartment, right?'

'Yes.' Nelson looked exhausted and ill. All the brightness had disappeared.

'Do you own a car, Mr Nelson?'

'Yes, I do.'

'Why didn't you drive it?'

'I wasn't sure where it was parked. Sometimes we have to park on Spadina when this street is crowded.'

'But why wouldn't you know where it was?'

'Because Jake was driving it that day.' The statement came out slowly and painfully.

'What kind of car is it?'

'A Jeep.'

'The one on the street now?'

'Yes.'

'When did you drive it again?'

'The next day, when Jake brought it back. He tried to kill me, didn't he?'

'You know him better than anyone. Would he do that?'

'He had the Jeep that night, didn't he? He went to the store. Now he's disappeared.'

'We've found him.'

'Where? *Where?*'

'I'll let you know after I've talked to him. When did you realize all this?'

'Right away. That was why I didn't want to see him again.'

'So you've known all along that Hauser might be our man.'

Nelson looked at Salter and his face twisted as he fought with his misery.

'I thought so, yes. But I didn't want to see him in prison for life. I talked to Julia about it and she agreed that the best thing was to try and forget about it and hope Jake was gone for good.' There were no tears, but his throat was jerking with the pain of holding them in.

'Did she? When did you talk to her?'

'All the time. She's the only one I can talk to.'

'Did you accuse your friend of trying to kill you?'

'Yes. The next day. He swore he didn't, of course, but he would, wouldn't he, especially after we knew Drecker was dead?'

Clocks were chiming in Salter's head. 'I'm going to see him now,' he said. 'I'll call you later and tell you if you can see him.'

'Don't hurt him, will you.'

Twice in one day was too much. 'For Christ's sake,' Salter shouted, really angry. 'We don't spend all our time beating up

220

people like you for fun.' Then he was sorry at the effect of his words as Nelson crumpled into his chair. Against his better judgment Salter continued. 'Look, Mr Nelson, right now I think you talk to other people too much when you should be talking to me. I'd like your word that you will not talk to anyone about this case, including your friend Julia, until I say okay. Then I'll tell you something.'

Nelson nodded two or three times as he wiped his face with his hands.

'Good. Right, then. Here it is. I do not believe your friend set fire to Drecker's store. I think I know who might have killed Drecker, but I don't know why or how. When I can figure those two out, I'll be able to do something. I may have the answers this afternoon.'

Now the look of relief on Nelson's face was harder to take, if possible, than the misery. 'I won't say a word, Inspector. I'll take the phone off the hook and lock the door,' he said. 'When can I see Jake?'

'I'll let you know,' Salter said, and left to drive to the hospital.

★   ★   ★

Hauser was in a private room to make guarding him simpler. Salter walked along the corridor until he came to the constable reading a magazine outside the door. He showed his identification and the policeman let him in. 'Not much to guard,' the officer said. 'He's not going anywhere.'

Hauser was lying back on his pillow, watching the door. Both eyes were black, and bandages covered his throat. His lips were swollen and bruised, and his hair had been shaved on the front of his scalp where another wound had been dressed. According to the report, he had three broken ribs and severe bruising on the abdomen where he had been kicked.

'What happened?' Salter asked.

Hauser reached beside his pillow for a pair of steel rimmed glasses. 'Who are you?' he asked.

He looked a wretched sight. His skin was mud-coloured and greasy, and his hair was scanty and dying. At his best he could not have been handsome, and the ugly glasses suggested he was indifferent to his looks. Now, swollen and bruised, he would be a real test of charity for any Samaritan, Salter thought. But Nelson loved him, which was no more or less mysterious than the attraction of some married couples to each other. The policeman identified himself. 'What happened?' he repeated.

'I was lonely. I went to a bar for some company and met a couple of queer-bashers. I've already described them, but you won't catch them. You never do.'

'We might,' Salter said. 'But I'm more interested in something else right now.'

'Drecker. I didn't kill him. I know Dennis thinks I did, but I didn't.'

'You were there about the time the fire was set,' Salter asserted.

'I guess I must have been. But I didn't set it.'

'Tell me what you did that night. In detail.'

'Dennis and I had a fight. You know that. Then he left, and I thought he went to the store, so I followed him there.'

'In the Jeep?'

'Yes. But he wasn't there when I arrived and I could see Drecker's truck parked out back, so I went back to Washington Avenue to wait for him. I waited all night, but he never showed up. Finally, I took off and came back next day. That's when Dennis decided I had tried to kill him.'

'So why did you disappear?'

'If Dennis believed it, you would. How could I prove I didn't? I was terrified.'

'Let's get back to the night. You drove to the store. Where did you park, on Bloor Street?'

'No. I went around the back to the laneway. I thought there would be parking space behind. But Drecker's truck was there, so I waited in the lane for about five minutes in case I had beaten Dennis to the store. Then I went back to Washington.'

'How? What route?'

'I went along the lane to the end, and then I went north for a block, then east for another block, then north again, then east—you know how all those one-way streets won't let you go where you want until you get to a major street?'

'Did you come out at Bloor?'

Hauser shook his head 'You can't get out to Bloor from that lane. I had to go all round the Annex before I could get back on to Spadina first.'

'How long did it take you?'

'About ten minutes. There was no traffic at that time. Why?'

'It's important. To you. Did you see anyone else, any other car, parked with anyone in it?'

'No. It would be nice, wouldn't it? But I didn't notice anything strange.'

'All right, Mr Hauser.' Salter stood up. 'I'll get back to you as soon as I can.'

'I didn't kill him, Inspector.'

'No. I know you didn't. But it looks bad, and I'll have to leave the guard on you for a little longer.'

'You mean that? You believe me?'

'Let's say I don't disbelieve you, and I hope I'm right.'

Hauser looked down at the bed. 'How is Dennis?' he asked, his voice a croak now.

'Upset. And asking after you, so the sooner I get on with this the better. Do you need anything?'

Hauser shook his head. 'Thank you,' he said.

★ ★ ★

From the pay-phone in the vestibule he called Sergeant Gatenby.

'Tell me again exactly what that anonymous caller said,' he asked.

'He said,' Gatenby began, reading his notes, 'I saw a Jeep, a silver one with the word RENEGADE on the side, tearing off along Bloor Street right after the fire.'

'West or east?'

There was a long pause.

'He said towards Spadina. That's east.'

'What sort of voice?'

'Male. Over thirty—not a kid, anyway. Sure of himself. Actually he sounded familiar, but I couldn't say why.'

I can. 'Okay, Frank. That's what I wanted. He won't call again, but if he does, get all the details you can. You know, play along with him.'

'Right you are. On to something, are you?'

'I think so, Frank. I think so. I'll call you later.'

Next Salter drove up Mount Pleasant Road to the American Motors' showroom. There he wandered around the cars parked outside until he found a Jeep, and crossed the road to look at it from the other side. He looked at it from all angles and various distances until he was satisfied. Two of the salesman from the showroom watched him closely. 'I'm in advertising,' Salter explained to them. 'Just trying out angles for a visual.' Darling, he thought, you've trapped yourself, you clever bastard. Now I've just got to figure out how to jump you.

He drove back down to the Metro Library on Yonge Street and spent an hour reading up the history of the Japanese in Canada, especially the wartime years. Finally he was ready to meet Gene Tanabe.

★ ★ ★

Jacob Harz opened the door himself and showed him into the living-room where a Japanese gentleman dressed in a grey flannel suit and wearing an open-necked white shirt was waiting for him.

'Mr Tanabe?'

The old man looked at Jacob Harz for guidance.

'Sit down, Inspector. We'll have some tea, then Gene can tell you his story.'

A woman in an apron brought in the tea-things, and Harz poured them all a cup, while Salter got a good look at Tanabe. Where old age had given Harz a broken, knobbly look, it had had the effect of drying and preserving the Japanese. His hands were large, with heavy, flat fingertips, but the rest of him had withered gently so that he reminded Salter (and here the policeman realized where his mind was leading him) of an old grasshopper, and a legend he had heard from a Grade Twelve English teacher.

Salter left his notebook in his pocket. Story

first, questions afterwards. 'Now, Mr Tanabe. What is your connection with Cyril Drecker?'

'I killed him, Inspector,' Tanabe said, quietly, impersonally, with a little smile.

'No, you didn't,' Harz said. 'He didn't, Inspector. Gene, tell the man your story, for God's sake.'

'Mr Harz,' Salter said. 'Why don't I listen to Mr Tanabe. Then later on you can comment.'

'Shut up, you mean?'

'That's right.'

'I won't let Gene hang himself.'

'Neither will I. Okay?'

'Okay,' Harz said. 'But Gene wants me to stay with him.'

'So do I. Now, Mr Tanabe. Your story.'

'The whole thing?' Tanabe's manner seemed to suggest a thousand years of history.

'Yes, please.'

'It starts in nineteen forty-two.'

'Start there, then. We've got all afternoon.'

The old man looked again at Harz, who nodded at him. He began. 'In nineteen forty-two I was living in Vancouver on Pandora Street. I was a cabinet maker and furniture restorer. Then the police came and told me I

228

had to move inland. I had nowhere to go. Fortunately I had no family, no wife or children, so I went to a place, a sort of ghost town they were sending people like me to, in the interior of the province. I had a lot of furniture in stock but they would not let me sell it because the local dealers complained it would depress the market, so I put it in storage. When I came back after the war it had all gone—stolen, I suppose. I took only some clothes and my tools so I could work.' The old man paused, and Harz fussed about him, refilling his teacup.

'I had a few personal things from the old country, although I was born in Canada, like you, Inspector.' A small rustle of life appeared in the quiet tale, a hint of passion.

'He's a nisei,' Harz explained. 'That means second-generation Japanese.'

Salter looked at Harz, who shrugged and picked up his teacup.

Tanabe cleared his throat. 'My parents were dead and I had no other family. These few things I put in a box and asked a friend to keep them for me.'

'George Kemp?'

'Yes. George was a good friend, and he was sorry for what was happening to me so he offered to look after anything I wanted to leave with him. I left him my box.'

'Did he know what was in it?'

'No. So I went off to this town and stayed there for a year. Then they moved me to a camp in Ontario, farther away from the coast. After another six months they said I could live on the outside if I stayed away from Vancouver. I wanted to work at my trade again.'

'That's when he came to me,' Harz said.

'Jacob took me in, and I worked for him and lived with his family until the war was over. As soon as I could I went back to Vancouver to start my business again. I became a dealer, now, though, as well, especially in Japanese art.'

'Gene is one of the best known in the business,' Harz said.

Whenever Harz spoke, Tanabe waited, smiling.

'When I returned I went immediately to my friend's house, but it was gone. Burned down, the neighbours said, soon after I left. No one knew where George was. He and his wife and baby had left the district. The neighbours told me that there was very little saved from the fire, so I forgot about my box. I never saw or heard of George again, but about a month ago I found some of my prints on sale.'

'At MacLeod's gallery?'

'Yes. I often buy things from him. He told me where these had come from and I called on the man. I bought my prints back from Mr MacLeod first.'

'You are sure they were yours?'

'Oh yes. Do you know anything about Japanese prints, Inspector?'

'Something, yes. I know they can be identified. So what did Drecker say?'

'First, I found my box on sale in the shop.'

'Do you still have it here in Toronto?' Salter held his breath. A varnished box in storage for forty years. It should yield perfect fingerprints—Drecker's, Nelson's, Murdrick's, Tanabe's, and Darling's. 'May I see it?'

'Of course. It is in the basement.' Tanabe got up without any of the awkwardness of age, and moved to the door. Harz waved them on. 'You go ahead, Gene. I can't run up and down the stairs.'

Tanabe led Salter down the stairs into the huge basement. A small part of the room was taken up with a furnace, and along one wall were ranged the usual laundry machines and tubs, but a corner of the room was evidently a workshop where Harz could still dabble at his old trade. There, on the main bench, was the box, glowing with a rich shine.

'You cleaned it up?' Salter asked.

'Yes. Beautiful, isn't it? I had very little to do so I completely refinished it. I want to keep it to remind me.' Tanabe took out a handkerchief and rubbed the lid softly.

So much for fingerprints. After Salter had sufficiently admired Tanabe's work, the two men returned upstairs.

Tanabe continued his story. 'Drecker was not at the store that first day. When I came back he was very unpleasant. He said the box had turned up as part of a lot brought in by a picker, and he had bought it for cash. He did not know who had sold it to him, he said. There was no more to be done. He would not even tell me who had bought the rest of my things. Why? But I felt Drecker was dishonest, and I wanted to find out why the box had turned up after forty years. I bought it back from Drecker. I knew it was mine but there was no point in arguing. I really wanted to find out if my old friend had sold it. In Vancouver, in nineteen forty-two, he was very good to me, and I trusted him. I had a happy memory of George.'

'So you went to look for him?'

'Yes. It wasn't very hard. I soon found out

about his daughter, Mrs Murdrick, who lives in Toronto. And then I found out about my box. George had saved it from the fire and he had kept it for me all those years in case I came back. He didn't let me down, not at all.' Tanabe looked happily at Salter.

'But his daughter did?'

'I don't think so. Did you talk to her?'

'Yes. She told me the box had been stolen from a garage sale they had after Kemp got sick.'

'Yes, that is what she thinks.'

'You believed her?'

'Yes. I believed she was telling the truth. She told me her father had kept it all those years and she was very upset that it was gone. Yes, I believed her. But I did not believe her husband, who seemed to be lying and angry with me. I did not believe Drecker, either, so I thought that Murdrick had sold the box to Drecker and told him that he had told his wife it was stolen.' Tanabe paused to allow Salter to speak.

'You couldn't prove it though, could you? It might just as easily have been as they said. Someone stole it and sold it to Drecker.'

'Then why did Drecker act so strange, so hostile?' Tanabe was teaching Salter now, leading him through a dialogue.

'All right. So what could you do?'

'Nothing for myself. But I decided to take a little revenge. I thought that with these people they would all try to cheat each other. Some of my prints have become quite valuable . . .'

'I know what MacLeod paid Drecker, and what you paid to get them back,' Salter interrupted.

'Yes? Well, I thought that maybe Drecker would have cheated Murdrick. So I went back to say goodbye to George and pretended to sympathize with Murdrick over losing "our" box. I told him how valuable the prints were. I exaggerated a little. I told him how happy I was to get them back even though I had had to pay so much for them. I told him Drecker probably got five thousand for them. Lucky Drecker, I said. That's how I killed him.'

'How?'

'Because my shot in the dark was right. I think that two days later Murdrick burned down Drecker's store because he had been cheated.'

Salter shook his head. 'Murdrick was in Montreal that night.'

Tanabe let out a sigh. 'Then it was an accident? Good. But it might have been my fault.'

'What did you expect to happen?'

'I thought Murdrick would perhaps demand some money from Drecker, perhaps assault him a little. But when I heard that Drecker was dead I got frightened. These people were more violent than I thought.'

'So you disappeared.'

'Yes.'

'Where did you go? We searched this town pretty carefully.'

'To Buffalo. I have some friends there. I was frightened to stay in Canada.'

'We serve and protect, Mr Tanabe. That's our motto. We would have looked out for you. But what, specifically, were you frightened of?'

'I thought if Murdrick would kill a man who was cheating him, he might kill me for exaggerating, if he found out.'

It was hard to believe. To do so, thought Salter, you had to get inside the skin of an old Japanese gentleman who had been made timid by his experience.

There was a long pause while the three races drank tea. Then Salter said, 'Murdrick didn't kill Drecker.'

Tanabe said, 'So you say. But I have just thought. You can hire people to do these things.'

'You need influence and money for that. Murdrick had neither. Someone did kill Drecker and I think I know who it was. Up until now I didn't know why. Now I think I know why, though from the start I figured it was a case of thieves falling out. I still can't prove it because there is a very good alibi to break, so what I'd like to do is to take a shot in the dark, like you did, Mr Tanabe. If it works, as I think yours did, then we'll catch him. Will you make another phone call to Murdrick, and tell him something?' Salter outlined the story he wanted told.

'Mr Salter, I am not interested in these people and I do not want anything more to do with them. I don't care who killed Drecker. You will have to find out by yourself.'

Harz said, 'The man is doing his job, Gene. What's there to say no to? Do what he asks.'

Salter stayed silent while Harz urged Tanabe to cooperate. He saw that his request had made Tanabe angry, or, perhaps, revealed the anger he always carried, and he felt the danger of saying the wrong word. Gradually Tanabe relaxed under Harz's pleading and finally agreed to make the call.

'Now?' he asked.

'No. We'll catch him at home, this evening. I'll have to set it up first, so I'll leave you now and come back at eight. Okay?'

'Why go away?' Harz said. 'Eat supper with us, Inspector. It's the sabbath. Please.'

What would a Jewish sabbath meal with a Japanese guest be like? Raw fish or rye? Bagels and seaweed? 'Thanks,' Salter agreed. 'I'd like that. One thing before we leave your story, Mr Tanabe. Why did Kemp make so little attempt to find *you* after the war, instead of carrying the box around for forty years. He didn't seem to try very hard.'

Tanabe looked embarrassed. 'That's what you and I would have done, Inspector, but I think George *liked* looking after the box for me. His daughter said that he told everyone about the box, and how he was keeping it for me. If he inquired after me, and perhaps found I was dead, (and I'm sure people suggested that to him) he might be able to sell the box, but his life would not be so interesting without it. George is a good man, and he isn't stupid, but he is not sophisticated, I think. The box was a sacred trust—it represented his honesty, our friendship, and the time when he went against mob opinion. Of course, he wanted me to come back and claim the box, but the

237

next best thing to that was having the box beside him, not selling it for a few dollars. Am I making any sense? I have often thought about it.'

It made a great deal of sense to Salter as he remembered his own impression of Kemp, the independent old Newfie who regarded Canada as another country, and his son-in-law, Murdrick the twister, as a typical Canadian. ('I gave me word to Gene, d'ye'see, and where I come from you can trust a fella's word.') Salter felt himself surrounded by honourable old men from another age, and he was surprised by the quick flash of an old adolescent regret that his own father did not inspire the same feeling.

No one said anything for a few moments. Then Salter asked to use the phone and called home. Angus answered.

'Mom phoned, too, Dad. She's working late. Don't worry. I'll take Seth out to McDonald's,' he said, one man to another. 'I'll use my own money. You can pay me back, and it's OK about the fishing. We'll go next weekend.'

Salter then called his office, telling Gatenby to wait for a later call, and to have two cars and four men standing by.

'Can I come?' Gatenby asked.

238

Salter laughed. 'You can direct field operations, Frank,' he said, and hung up.

While they waited for supper, Esther served them more tea, and Harz and Tanabe took the opportunity of a new audience to reminisce about the wartime days in Toronto when the two outsiders lived together. At one point Harz asked Salter if he would like some whisky. 'We have whisky, don't we, Esther, for the Inspector? No? Brandy then. Have some brandy. Esther, give the man some brandy.' Again Salter refused. Harz and his daughter then began discussing the various others liquors they could offer the policeman, and Tanabe said, 'They have a little folksong, Mr Salter . . .'

Harz cut him off quickly. 'No, no, no,' he protested. 'My mother used to say that, a long time ago. Now I know as many drunks as Mr Salter does. You shouldn't say things like that.' He was very embarrassed, but Tanabe smiled like an ancient schoolboy. The old grasshopper could still chirp.

Salter suspected that the exchange was something to do with the way gentiles drank.

Esther announced dinner, and they sat down. It was back to Grade Six for Salter, sitting still and watching his manners. Would they put on little hats?

First the daughter lit two candles and recited something formal.

'That is the blessing,' Tanabe said.

The first course seemed to be some kind of fish balls. Tanabe passed him a dish of something red. 'Horseradish,' he explained. 'You eat it with the fish.'

Probably a compromise, Salter thought, because of Tanabe. One Japanese dish (raw fish) and one Jewish. My old dad should be here for this. He tried some of the fish and horseradish, and while it was not bad it was not wonderful, either.

'Did you invent this combination, Miss Harz?' he asked.

'No', she said. 'Horseradish is traditional with gefilte fish.'

'Maybe the Inspector would like some beer,' the ever courteous Harz suggested. 'Esther, get Mr Salter some beer. We got some during the summer. It's in the basement.'

Salter stopped them, insisting he did not want any, and Esther served them some chicken soup. This was delicious; it was followed by chicken stew with dumplings. Salter asked if this dish was traditional, also.

'This is a Reform household,' Tanabe said. 'But what we are having is a traditional

Friday night meal. Jacob quit going to the synagogue during the war, and raised Esther as an agnostic. Now she is more orthodox than he ever was. She would like him to observe all the rituals.' Tanabe seemed to be teasing Esther slightly. The daughter said nothing, but smiled tolerantly at him.

Finally Esther served some fruit salad without any icecream, and afterwards they went back to the living-room for more tea. Salter, slightly more relaxed, paused to look at a tapestry on the wall.

'That's very old,' Harz said. 'It portrays God's love of the universe.'

'Hebrew?' Salter asked.

'It came from Persia,' Harz said.

Salter gave up, and just concentrated on keeping his eyes and ears open for stories to tell Annie. When he finished his tea he went to work, calling his office and explaining to Gatenby what he wanted. 'Two men at the back, two in front, all of them in plain cars and out of sight, and a car following in case I'm wrong. Okay. In an hour. At seven-thirty. Right.'

While they waited Harz prodded Tanabe to tell Salter the story of his treatment in the war, but Salter had spent time in the library and he grew slightly restive at Tanabe's

241

continual reference to the police forces who moved the Japanese out of their homes.

'Mr Tanabe,' he said. 'The mounties didn't make the decision to move you. That was a political decision. The federal government, the provincial government and the local council. One local MP was particularly active—a guy with a Scots name.'

'They all looked alike to us, Inspector,' Tanabe said.

'Maybe, but things might have been even rougher if one of the senior mounties hadn't dragged his feet, trying to stop what was going on. He knew the Japanese were no threat and he said so.'

'The effect was the same to us.' Tanabe's tone was uninterested. Salter was having no effect.

'Yes,' he said, 'but behind the cops were the politicians, looking for votes. It's usually that way.'

'Why don't we talk about something else?' Harz pleaded.

There was an embarrassed silence for a while, until Harz asked Salter to tell them how he had learned about Tanabe, and the talk turned to MacLeod's gallery and Japanese prints.

Finally it was time, and Tanabe got ready

to dial the number Salter had given him. 'Do you really think he will believe this, Mr Salter? If he thinks about it, surely he will suspect something.'

'Murdrick is not a thinker, Mr Tanabe. We are trying to make him panic. If it doesn't work, I'll have to go at it another way, but if it does work it will save me a hell of a lot of trouble.'

Tanabe dialled the number and waited. Then, 'Mr Murdrick, this is Gene Tanabe. Do not hang up. Listen. This is very important to you. Please. Listen. The police have the box, my box. They have been questioning me all day and now they have just taken it away for testing. I told them I do not care now who stole the box, if it *was* stolen, but they are very interested in whoever had the box lately. I don't know why. I am calling you just in case. Because your wife and her father looked after it for so long. I thought maybe you did sell the box, and I am phoning to tell you that I want to forgive and forget. But the police are being very persistent.' Here Tanabe paused, and the other men could hear Murdrick shouting. 'Then you have nothing to worry about, Mr Murdrick. I am very glad. Please give my regards to your wife and your father-in-law.

243

Goodbye, Mr Murdrick.' Tanabe broke the connection immediately and put down the receiver.

'Very nice, Mr Tanabe,' Salter said. 'That should be it.'

'What if Murdrick just phones, Inspector? You got his line tapped?' Harz inquired.

Salter shook his head. 'He won't phone in front of his wife. And if we've scared him, he'll want to talk to Darling right away.'

The phone rang again, and Salter answered it. 'Right,' he said. 'We're on our way.' He stood up. 'Murdrick is getting into his truck,' he said. 'I'll see you later.'

*　　　*　　　*

Salter raced along Chaplin Crescent, slowing slightly at all the new stop signs, crossed Yonge Street and drove along Davisville Avenue to Mount Pleasant Road, where he turned towards downtown.

The radio spoke. 'Suspect travelling west on Queen Street.'

Salter was now travelling south on Jarvis and he continued on to Queen and turned east into Cabbagetown.

The radio spoke again. 'Suspect now travelling north on Parliament.'

Now they were right behind the police car. Salter turned north on Parliament and saw the car about a block ahead. In front of it was Murdrick's truck, paused at a stop-light. he spoke into the radio. 'Take it easy. I've got the house staked out, and I can see him. When he stops just keep circling the block until we need you.'

Murdrick turned left and Salter followed. When the truck stopped, Salter parked fifty feet away. Murdrick ran up to the door and banged on it with his fist until he was let in.

Salter spoke into the radio. 'Give them five minutes, exactly. I'll take us in the front door. I want them separated right away and taken down to the station. Then we'll search the house.'

Five minutes later Salter knocked at the door. When the door opened, he said, 'Mr Darling? I'd like a word with you.' Darling tried to close the door, but two policemen carried him with them as they moved into the house. There was a small scuffle when Murdrick tried to get through the back door, but the two men were soon installed in the police cars and taken away.

CHAPTER SIX

Murdrick and Darling were being held in adjoining rooms. Salter began with Murdrick and it took him very little time to uncover the tiler's involvement. He had arranged for Darling to take the box on the day of the yard sale, and Darling had delivered it to Drecker. That much he admitted to in a rush in order to deny any involvement in the fire, which he could not have been involved in anyway, as he pointed out, six or seven times, belligerently, pleadingly, and finally in a continuous whine, because he was in Montreal.

'But you knew Darling could have set the fire,' Salter pointed out.

'He could have; he might have; I don't know anything about that,' Murdrick repeated over and over again, abandoning Darling immediately.

'So you stole the box and profited from the theft? Right?' Salter asked, adopting a quasi-legal tone.

'I got two hundred dollars for it,' shouted Murdrick. 'Two fucking hundred.'

'Darling swindled you, then.'

246

'I guess so. No. I don't *know*. He says he only got four hundred from Drecker,' Murdrick said, shouting still in frustration and fear.

'Why did you go over to Darling's tonight, then?'

'To warn him. Because I didn't know *what* was going on, and when that old Jap told me how much Drecker had got and then called me to tell me you fellas were on to the box, I figured I'd better let Darling know.'

'You didn't want to let your old pal down?' Salter jeered. 'Or you figured we could nail you as an accessory after the fact to arson and murder?'

'I didn't have nothing to do with the fire.'

'But you thought Darling might have, didn't you?'

'Yes, I bloody did.'

'Why?'

'Because of the state he got into when he found out how much the stuff in the box was worth.'

'What did he say?'

'I don't remember.'

'Threats? Promises to get Drecker?'

'I don't remember. All I remember is he was in a bloody rage.'

They went round it for an hour. Salter had

247

got what he wanted in the first five minutes, but he pressed Murdrick to the limit before he got him to sign a statement about the theft and Darling's involvement. Then he told Murdrick he was holding him for theft and for further questioning about the arson, and had him locked up for the night.

Before he moved on to Darling he went over the case with Gatenby to clear his mind, and got a useful suggestion from the sergeant. He took Murdrick's statement into Darling and read it to him while Gatenby sat by, taking notes.

'So, Mr Darling, we have you, on the evidence of the box itself, and on Murdrick's statement, on a charge of theft over two hundred dollars. Looks as though you are going to need one of your professional friends pretty soon.'

'Drecker set it up,' Darling said immediately. 'He was the fence, and he's dead.'

Salter smiled. 'He'd covered himself,' he said. 'He listed the box with us when you brought it in to him, in case it was stolen. Said it had been sold to him by a casual vendor. You. R. Darling of Church Street. I've known that for a week.'

'That cunning bastard,' Darling cried, as

he realized how careful Drecker had been.

'Now let's move on. When did you decide to burn down Drecker's store?'

Darling exploded. 'What the hell are you bastards up to?' he shouted. 'Sure I stole the box with Murdrick, but I'm not a bloody arsonist, mister, and you know it. My wife and the people I was playing cards with that night can testify as to where I was. You won't get me on that one. I'm covered.'

Salter pressed the point in several ways and watched Darling's confidence build as the policeman found no new chink to probe. Then he said, 'Do you read detective stories, Mr Darling?'

'What's that got to do with anything?'

'I'm just asking. You don't have to answer.'

'Sometimes. Sure.'

Salter nodded. 'Do you know what a cliché is?' A recent case had taken Salter into the academic world where he had heard a lot about clichés from the experts.

'Of course I know what a cliché is,' Darling responded, offended and arrogant.

'Well, let me tell you then that you've been reading too many stories. Your alibi is a cliché, Mr Darling, one of the oldest in the trade.'

'What the hell are you talking about?' Darling responded, frightened but still noisy.

'The trick of putting the clocks back.' Salter pretended to consult his notebook. 'According to you *and* your wife, on the night of the fire you woke her up, pointed out the time.' Salter searched for the right word. 'Did your stud act, pointed out the time *again*, and went back to sleep. Right?'

'That's right.'

'I'll tell you what really happened, shall I? You went down to Drecker's store from your card game—I've talked to the professional people you played with and they confirm your story—set fire to it, drove home, put the clock back an hour, showed your wife the time, performed, pointed out the time again, waited until she was asleep, then put the clock forward. As I say, a cliché, typical of a clever-dick mind.'

Darling went white. 'Jesus Christ. You bastard. You *are* trying to frame me.'

'I'm trying to get you to make it simple for me.'

'Never, you sonofabitch. No way.'

Salter hardened his pose. 'I mean, save me a lot of trouble. Let me tell you something. It's very tough to get out of a fire clean. You always take something with you. We will pick

250

your house and shop apart until we find something you took away from Drecker's that night. A bit of dust from his basement floor on your shoe; a fleck of paint from the wall. It'll be there, and we'll find it. But it may take us a long time. You could save us a lot of trouble.'

To his dismay, Salter saw some of the tension go out of Darling.

'You can search all you want, but I wasn't there, so you won't find anything you haven't planted. I wasn't there.'

Salter brought up his last gun. 'Then why did you try and frame Jake Hauser?'

Once more Darling went pale, but this time there was real fright in his voice, as he said, 'What the fuck are you talking about?'

'I'm talking about the phone call you made about the silver Jeep you saw leaving the fire.'

'What phone call? What Jeep? What are you talking about?'

Now Salter felt sure of himself. 'We have a voice-print of the call,' he said (this was Gatenby's suggestion) 'and we can match it as easily as we can match your fingerprints on the box. So why did you try and frame Hauser?'

Darling looked for a way out, then

251

accepted the charge.

'Well, he did it, didn't he?'

'Did he?'

'Sure he did. Those two queers had a fight so Nelson's pal tried to kill him. It's bloody obvious, except to you.'

'Who told you? Julia Costa?'

Darling was silent.

Salter nodded. Even Nelson thought so, and he shared all his thoughts with Julia Costa. 'So you wanted to help us out, like a good citizen, like your professional friends would have done,' Salter said. 'Instead of reporting your suspicions to us, you made up a nice little story to wrap it all up for us, right? You might be interested to know that your story was so bloody silly that I was able to prove Hauser couldn't have done it just by checking your story. So now, why the phone call? I know the answer, of course. To divert suspicion, as they say in those stories of yours.'

'No, it goddam wasn't,' Darling roared. 'I didn't set fire to the goddam store. All I was worried about was getting nabbed for stealing the lousy box. Sure Drecker swindled me . . .'

'And you swindled Murdrick.'

'I took more risks than he did. But *I didn't*

set fire to his store. But you were so hung up on that box I figured you might find out eventually how it got stolen, and I figured that if you got Hauser first, you'd be happy and forget about the box. Christ, it looked obvious to me.'

'Just like you do to me.'

'Never, mister. Never. I didn't kill him, I tell you.'

And there they stuck. Salter tried all the tricks, including getting a colleague to play Mutt to his Jeff, but Darling was immovable. He was badly frightened as he saw the case against him, but he found a certainty from somewhere to hang on to and nothing would shift him.

At midnight Salter gave up. He charged Darling formally with the same offences as Murdrick, and went home to bed, where he lay awake for most of the night, replaying the mental tape of Darling's interview.

★   ★   ★

'Are you going to have another go at him now?' Orliff asked him the next morning. He was in the office when Salter arrived and the two men had gone over the case together.

'I guess so. Then we'll take his house

253

apart.'

'You certain of yourself, Charlie?'

'Yesterday I was, but last night I got a feeling from Darling that there's something I haven't thought of.'

Orliff stiffened. 'I told you, leave the feelings and the hunches to Sherlock Holmes. Just get all the facts and see what they add up to. Now, do you think he did it from what you've found out so far, or not?'

Salter looked out the window. 'I think I do,' he said.

'Then go and get him. By the way, whose idea was it to tell him we had a voice-print. That was cute.'

'Gatenby,' Salter said, still brooding.

'Sly bastard. And this clock stuff. Cliché or not, it sounds okay to me. It'll make you look pretty at the trial if you can nail him.'

'If I'm right, I'll nail him,' Salter said, and picked up his notes to go back to questioning his two suspects.

★   ★   ★

But Salter was wrong. He had spent ten more minutes with Murdrick, trying to get him to recall every word Darling had ever spoken, when Gatenby poked his head round the

254

door.

'Something funny here, sir,' he said. 'You should look at it.'

It was a report from the Fire Marshal's office: someone had set fire to Darling's store the night before. Salter stared at the report, sensing that his whole case against Darling was coming to pieces.

'Does this screw it all up?' Gatenby asked gently.

Salter picked up a pencil and started listing. 'Murdrick and Darling are in jail; Tanabe is in the clear; Hauser is in hospital. So who have we got?'

'Maybe a coincidence,' Gatenby offered. 'Or a good way to give Darling an alibi.'

'Right, Frank, right,' Salter said immediately. 'That must be it. Who then? Not Nelson, that's for sure. Julia Costa? Mrs Drecker? One of the wives? Darling's wife, maybe, not Murdrick's.' Salter thrashed around, looking for an accomplice of Darling's. He pulled the phone towards him and dialled the Fire Marshal's office, asking to speak to the investigator of the fire.

'Smudge-pots,' he cried, after listening for a few moments. He listened for a few more moments. 'Okay. Thanks.' He put the phone down. 'Somebody put smudge-pots in

Darling's store last night while Darling was here. Smudge-pots are what construction workers use in the bush to keep off mosquitoes. No damage, just smoke. What the fuck.' Salter gazed out the window.

Five minutes later Gatenby spoke, but Salter waved him to silence. After a good ten minutes more he slumped in his chair and began to scratch the top of his head with both hands. Then he put his hands over his ears, and shut his eyes.

Gatenby looked at him worriedly. 'Okay, sir?' he asked.

Salter got up. 'I'm okay, Frank. Put your coat on. We've got a call to make.'

In the car he explained to the sergeant exactly what had happened. 'Stay downstairs when we get there,' he said. 'I won't need any help inside. This is not going to be much fun.'

He parked alongside the house with his wheels up on the sidewalk. When he knocked on the door, Mrs Murdrick answered immediately, her face muddy with lack of sleep. 'What do you want now?' she wailed in misery, when she recognized Salter. 'You've got my husband in jail.'

From the top of the stairs George Kemp spoke. 'I think it's meself he's after,' he said.

'Come on up, Inspector, while I put me coat on.' He stood majestically on his short legs, holding open the door of his room in invitation.

Salter climbed the stairs and entered the old man's room. Kemp closed the door and the two men sat down. They waited for a minute, then Salter spoke.

'I have to warn you . . .' he began.

The old man waved his hand slowly. 'You can forget all that,' he said. 'I did it; I'm not sorry I did it; I'm sorry for the fella who died, but that was no part of me intentions. I just wanted that bunch of twisters to pay for stealing the box I had kept safe for forty years. Now Gene will know how I felt about it, anyway.'

'How did you know it was Drecker and Darling? Your son-in-law never told you, surely?'

'I've bin follerin' the case step be step from the beginning,' Kemp said. 'Listen.'

Downstairs the telephone was ringing. The two men listened while Mrs Murdrick answered a call for her husband and told the caller that Murdrick had gone away for a few days. Every word came clearly through the floor.

'They built these houses of plywood,'

Kemp said.

'So you knew that Darling took the box and passed it to Drecker?'

'I had me suspicions from the first, but when Gene came and told me he'd found it, I assumed then that it had got into Drecker's hands by accident. But then the twister downstairs got a bit nervous and started making phone calls while I listened in.' He pointed to the floor. Now his face was definitely splitting; his mouth was open a little wider at one side than the other and a wedge-shaped gleam of yellow teeth showed through. 'Then I heard Gene telling him about the money Drecker had got for them pictures, and after Gene left he waited until me daughter went out shopping and then all bloody hell broke loose downstairs. Shoutin' at Darling on the phone he was—you didn't need any extension.'

'So you drove out to Drecker's store and set fire to it. How? Where did you get the keys?'

'I didn't need any keys. Just a length of half-inch copper pipe, a funnel and a drop of white gas. They are all in me truck still. You'll need them for evidence.'

Salter found it hard to believe. 'You stuck a pipe through the window, poured gas down

258

it, and then lit it?'

'That's right. One of the windows was covered over with a bit of plastic. It was easy as stealing pennies from a blind man.'

'What did you use for a fuse? We didn't find anything.'

Kemp beamed. 'Fooled you there, did I? Well, I'll tell yez. The week before, I'd taken the little lad over to Centre Island to one of them picnics. They had a lot of fireworks there, and they come to mind when I was looking for a fuse. You know them sparklers we used to have as kids? You can still buy them in Chinatown and I bought a packet on the Saturday. I chucked one in first and let the gas reach it. Made a dandy fuse, that did.'

'Jesus Christ,' Salter said. 'You could have blown yourself up, you know that?'

'I've been using naphtha for sixty years, mister, and I'm still here.'

'But didn't you think that we might have suspected your son-in-law?'

'Ah. That's why I did it when he was in Montreal. I drove him to the station meself before I went over to Drecker's. I thought of it, right enough.'

Salter thought to himself: That's it. When Mrs Murdrick had told him of the family outing to Montreal, he had assumed it included Kemp. He never checked, though. Just forgot about them all after that. Jesus Christ.

'We were bound to track you down eventually,' Salter said, to keep the old man talking.

Kemp cleared his throat and sniffed, twisting his face to open up all the passages. 'I don't know about that, Mister. Some of the polis I've known in this country couldn't track a wounded elephant through six feet of snow. Anyway, youse are forgettin', I didn't plan to kill that fella; I just wanted to set the cat among the pigeons, d'ye see? I thought if there was a little fire in Drecker's basement, and me son-in-law away in Montreal, then Drecker would jump to the conclusion that Darling had done it, and those two would have a go at each other. That's all I planned. A little back payment to the whole gang of them for taking Gene's box away. A little bit of a frame-up, like.'

A little bit of a frame-up. Just like Tanabe. A little bit of revenge. 'Your son-in-law and Darling and Drecker were all in it together,' Salter said. 'Why take it out on Drecker?'

'Well, me son-in-law is stupid, d'ye see, so Darling and Drecker swindled him easy enough, and then Drecker swindled

Darling—gave him four hundred dollars for stuff worth thousands, he was the only one really profitin'—Drecker, I mean. I figured that if I could make him pay, then I'd be satisfied. As I say, I didn't mean to kill him.'

'You're a hard man, George,' Salter said eventually.

'He made me let down me friend,' Kemp said. 'After forty years.'

There was nothing left, except, 'How did you ketch on to me in the end?' Kemp asked. 'That was smart of you,' he added generously.

'After last night it wasn't hard. All I needed was to find a plumber who wasn't in jail, someone who knew about white gas and smudge-pots.'

'How's that?'

'Smudge-pots. The kind steam-fitters and plumbers use up north. You keep *them* in your truck, too?'

'There's a couple left still.'

'But why smudge-pots? They wouldn't set fire to anything, would they?'

'Haven't you figured that out yet? One—' here Kemp stubbed a finger like a banana into his palm—'I wanted to cause a lot of smoke damage. Two: I didn't want anyone hurt this time. Three: smudge-pots or no, I heard me son-in-law phoning Darling last night, after he got a call from Gene, d'ye see. I can put two and two together and I knew it might look pretty bad for Darling. I've killed one man, hangashore that he was, and I wanted to rightify it. I didn't want another going to prison for me act, so I figured if Darling's place caught fire while you was having at him with your billy knockers, he'd be in the clear.'

Salter stood up. 'We'd better go,' he said.

Kemp put on his jacket and a flat cloth cap, and preceded Salter down the stairs. His daughter stood in the hall, silent and terrified. Kemp gave her an awkward kiss on the cheek. 'I'm going down to the cop-shop to help them with their inquiries,' he said. 'Don't upset yourself.'

From upstairs came the sound of a toilet flushing and a child's voice calling for his grandfather.

'Let's go before the little fella sees us,' Kemp said quickly.

Inside the car, he settled himself down and addressed Gatenby. 'How are you, Officer?' he asked.

'Fine,' Gatenby said, nonplussed. 'How are you, Mr Kemp?'

'Not bad, considering,' Kemp said. Then:

262

'How much do you think I'll get for this little lot?' he asked.

It was a question that had occurred to Salter. 'I don't know, George, I don't know,' he said eventually.

'Well, as the man said, I'll do as much as I can, but me infarction will probably take care of most of it.' And he laughed.

★　　★　　★

Before Salter went home he had a personal call to make, in Forest Hill. Harz and Tanabe were both at home, and Harz greeted him enthusiastically.

'All wrapped up, Inspector?'

'Yes, it is.' And Salter told the story. As he got to the point of his discovery of Kemp's involvement, Tanabe anticipated him and made a sighing noise, a tiny cry of misery.

'George?' he asked. 'My friend George? He did it?' He felt for a chair behind him and sat down.

Harz moved over to him. Salter explained how, and as far as he knew, why, Kemp had done it.

Tanabe stared at Salter, but turned to Harz when he spoke. 'It was my fault,' he said. 'George did it for me.'

'No, no, Gene,' Harz said. 'George did it for himself. Right. Inspector?'

Salter grabbed at this. 'I'm sure of it, Mr Harz.'

'How is George?' Harz asked.

'He seems fine, Mr Harz. I'll arrange for you to see him as soon as possible. I'll call you.'

'Good, good,' Harz said. 'I'll call my lawyer now.'

Salter got up to go. 'Goodbye, Mr Harz,' he said. 'Mr Tanabe.'

Harz came forward to show him to the door, but Tanabe just sat there looking at his hands for help.

★   ★   ★

There was enough distraction at home to keep Salter occupied until the evening, but by nine o'clock Annie was watching television and he was staring at the wall. She kept her eye on him until they went to bed, then slowly she got him talking. After a while Salter stopped justifying himself and began to speak calmly about his prejudice against people like Darling, to treat it objectively. When he started yawning, Annie shut up and concentrated on staying awake until he began to snore.

★   ★   ★

'Plumbers,' Salter said to Orliff later. 'I got stuck on the idea that we were looking for a plumber, and all the rest fell into place, the wrong place. I might have sent Darling up, you know that?'

'Don't sweat about it, Charlie. I warned you about tunnel vision, but you got there in the end. If you hadn't figured out that Darling made that phone call you wouldn't have pulled him in, and the old man might never have acted. Sounds to me like the old fella would have come forward anyway if we'd charged anyone else. Nice old guy. And you couldn't have found any evidence on Darling.'

'The only one with the know-how and no alibi. I assumed he was in Montreal with the rest of the family, but he only went as far as Union Station. Not very bright, was it?'

'I told you, don't sweat about it. Next time, though, don't let any little hunches get into the act. If you hadn't liked Kemp so much, maybe you'd have checked up on him earlier. And the same goes for Darling. You didn't like him, did you? What happened to

265

the two gays, by the way?'

'Nelson is taking over the shop, in partnership with Mrs Drecker.'

'And his friend?'

'He and Nelson have split up. Nelson *did* think that Hauser tried to kill him, and Hauser finds that hard to forgive.'

'That's too bad.' Orliff made a final note. 'And this Julia Costa? The friendly neighbourhood tart? She outside it all?'

'Oh yes. She's had it with plumbers, though.'

Orliff laughed. 'Now Charlie, listen to this. The Deputy wants to know if you want back in administration. While you are thinking about that, think about staying here with me. Special assignment. The old man is agreeable and I like having you around. I get everything that doesn't fit the regular squads, and I help out during rush periods. What do you say?'

Salter considered. Orliff was in many ways an ideal boss, without affection, malice, envy or fear. He did his job scrupulously and well, and watched the politicians on the Force manoeuvre and strain for position while he sat still, moving upwards into the spaces created by the internecine struggles in the organization, all the while looking after his own men.

'I'll stay here,' Salter said.

Orliff nodded. 'What about old Frank? We'll shift him out, eh? Get you a real sergeant. Who would you like?'

Salter shook his head. 'No. I'll keep Frank. I think he likes working with me and I'm used to him now. Besides—' here Salter the paranoiac confessed his real need—'I can trust him.'

'Right. You tell him, will you?' Orliff nodded to show the interview was over.

★　　　★　　　★

Wednesday evening. Annie had taken the boys to a movie, and Salter was in the back yard, looking at one of Angus's magazines which he had found at the bottom of the pile of old newspapers waiting to be put out for garbage.

Then, first one, then two wasps appeared, until a little swarm had materialized around him.

Right, he thought. He finished the rest of his beer, put the magazines in the garbage can, and climbed the stairs to the third floor. There he sat and looked at the screen door for a long time, then got out the magnifying-glass that came with the dictionary they had received for joining the book club. Through this he could see, as clearly as anything, the prongs that held the broken wheel. On his wife's dressing-table he found a nail file and a pair of eyebrow tweezers. With these he opened the prongs, lifted out the wheel, and dropped in the new wheel, easy as pie. He lifted the door on to its track, using the nail file to depress the wheel on the top of the door, and the door slid neatly into its grooves. He tested it gently, then firmly, and the door rolled smoothly in its track, just as if it had never been broken.

His family arrived home a few minutes later, and Salter just had time to get settled in front of the television with a fresh beer before they walked in.

When the boys had been hustled off to bed, Annie said, 'Look what I bought today.' She showed him a can of 'Hornet Death'. 'All you have to do is spray this stuff on the nest and it's guaranteed to kill all the inhabitants in thirty seconds.'

Salter nodded approvingly. 'I've fixed the door,' he said, over his shoulder. 'No problem.'

'Wow!' Annie said. 'I should go out more often. Oh, I've got a bit of news for you.'

This in her 'by-the-way' voice. 'I overheard Angus and Seth talking about sex tonight.'

'Seth!' Salter yelled. 'He's eleven, for God's sake.'

'Think back, Charlie.'

'What was Angus telling him?'

'He was telling him not to worry. It was all normal, what was happening.'

Salter gaped at her. Then he smiled. 'So, I don't have to take Angus fishing,' he said.

'Oh, Charlie. You were supposed to go *last* weekend.'

'Okay, okay. I was just joking. Don't worry. We're going.'

'Good,' she said. 'You never know. You might even enjoy it.'

EPILOGUE

They fished for two hours, catching a few small pickerel and some bass, and then Angus reeled in. 'I think I'll just sit here for a bit,' he said.

He's bored, Salter thought. Huckleberry Finn would have been as happy as if he'd been on salary, but my son is bored stiff. Salter got out the lunch of sandwiches he had made, and after they had eaten he started moving them upstream again, towards the cabin. The afternoon wore on slowly until Angus said, 'How long do you usually stay out, Dad?' and Salter gave up. He was now in an ugly mood, and yet aware enough of Annie's voice in his ear to try and blame himself for it. They docked at the cabin at five, and Angus disappeared inside. By the time Salter had tidied up the boat and joined him in the cabin, the boy was once again sitting on his bunk looking at a magazine.

'Start the fire, will you?' Salter asked him.

'How?'

'With paper, and little sticks, then bigger sticks and then logs,' Salter said.

'Where can I find any wood?'

Salter pointed through the window. 'Out there,' he said.

Angus went outside and came back a few minutes later with two sticks in his hand. 'This is all I could find,' he said.

Salter led him to the window. 'Out there,' he said, 'is maybe two hundred square miles of virgin forest with maybe twenty dead and fallen trees to the acre. Now get the hatchet and go out and bring back some wood.'

Angus went out again and eventually returned with an armload of wood, some of which was dry enough to be useful, and Salter showed him how to lay the fire in the stove. Angus moved to his task while Salter started the Coleman stove in the kitchen. In a few minutes the cabin was full of smoke. Salter opened the damper in the stove chimney, and then opened all the windows.

'Can I go for a swim, now?' the boy asked, not looking at his father.

'Of course you can. But go and get some more wood first. The fire is almost out already.'

Angus ran out and brought back another armful of wood which he dumped by the stove, then changed quickly into his trunks and disappeared. Salter waited for a minute, then walked out to the porch in time to see the boy dive in and start to swim across the river. At least he can swim, Salter thought. Better than I can.

By the time the chili was hot, Angus had returned and dried himself, and they ate supper in silence. Suddenly Angus said, 'Why did you become a policeman, Dad?'

Salter considered his reply. He knew, or thought he knew, that he was becoming a slight embarrassment to Angus, surrounded as he was at his posh school by the sons of surgeons and stockbrokers. He said, 'Because

I needed a job and it seemed like a good idea.'

'Do you still like it?'

Again Salter considered.

'Yes, I do,' he said. 'That's what I am, a policeman, the way other people are sailors and farmers, and even dentists, I guess. Why? Does it bother you?'

'No. Mum said you got very depressed by your last case.'

'Did she? Well she's right, I did, but I'll get over it.'

'Did you mess it up?'

Salter considered the question while Angus watched him closely. 'I went after the wrong guy, maybe because I didn't like him. I did like the guy who did it,' he said eventually.

'Mum said you got the right guy in the end.'

'Eventually, yes.'

'You're usually right, aren't you?'

Salter excused this piece of blatant flattery, and said nothing, wondering what Angus was working up to.

There was silence for a few moments. Then Angus said, 'I don't want to be a cop.'

'Good. What *do* you want?' At least they were talking.

'I don't know.'

'No ideas at all?'

The boy was silent for a while. Then: 'An actor maybe.' He looked cautiously at his father.

'So I hear. On the stage?'

'Sure. Did Mum tell you?'

'She mentioned something, yes. It's a hard life,' Salter said, who knew nothing about it.

'I don't care. Mum said she didn't mind.'

Did she? Salter thought. 'I don't mind either, son. I don't care what you do. Why didn't you tell me before?'

'I thought you might make fun of me, like you do with cricket and stuff.'

Salter was silent, feeling slightly sick.

'Well, I wouldn't,' he said. More was needed, though. 'You know why your mother doesn't mind? Because she loves you and wants you to do whatever will be satisfying for you. I feel the same way.' There. Nearly.

'Could we play some Scrabble?' Angus asked suddenly.

Salter loved playing Scrabble, but Angus had never shown any interest. Warily he asked, 'You don't like the game much do you?'

'No, but Mum said I should ask you.'

'Did she?' Salter shook his head. 'No, it's no fun unless you're a maniac for it like me

273

and your mother. No, let's clean up, get some more wood, and just read. This is the best reading place I know. A fishing cabin, I mean.'

'Okay. Can I have a beer?'

'No.'

'Why not?'

'It's against the law at your age, and you really are too young.'

'I've drunk beer before.'

'I know. And you've read skin books, too. So now you know about drinking and fucking.' I sound just like Gatenby's father, he thought. 'But you're still too young and you can wait a while for the big time. In the meantime, don't ask me for beer and don't bring skin books into the house. If you want to know anything, I'll try and tell you unless you get too personal.'

Angus gave a lop-sided grin, and that was that. They washed the dishes and settled down to read.

The next morning, either Angus had drawn strength from the tiny bond they had created, or the bond had disappeared. When Salter had the boat organized, he told Angus to hurry up.

Angus shook his head. 'I don't want to go fishing. Do you mind?'

'Why? Something wrong?'

'No. I just don't like it.'

'We could fish just around here. You could come in any time you want.'

'I JUST DON'T WANT TO GO FISHING. I DON'T WANT TO SIT IN THAT FUCKING BOAT ALL DAY.'

'All right, all right. So what are you going to do? *I'm* going fishing.'

'I'll be okay. There's stuff I can do. You go ahead.'

'You want to go home?'

'NO! You go fishing. Go on! I'll be fine.'

Salter looked at the boy who had once more picked up a magazine. Right, he thought, I will. 'Don't go swimming until I get back,' he said.

'All right.'

Salter turned upstream this time to a falls about three miles away. He had a perfect day. He found a shoal of pickerel that lasted for two hours, then he fished the shoreline for the rest of the day, looking for bass, eating Mars bars and drinking beer. Eventually he came in sight of the cabin again and saw Angus sitting on the dock in his bathing trunks. As he approached, the boy watched him calmly, then caught the prow of the boat and tied it up.

'Catch any?' he asked.

'Enough,' Salter said. 'Have you been sunbathing all day?' He didn't want to get into an argument, but he couldn't keep the irritation out of his voice.

'Nope,' the boy said. 'I've been working.' Salter looked more closely at him and saw that his hands and arms were covered in superficial cuts. There were scratches on his legs and even one or two on his face.

'Doing what?' Salter asked.

'I'll show you. Right now, I'm dying for a swim. Okay.'

'Okay.'

'Stay here, then. On the dock. Don't go to the cabin.'

Salter waited wonderingly as the boy dived in, swam out halfway, then raced back and pulled himself on to the dock.

They walked back to the cabin, and Angus said, 'There!'

'Where?'

'The wall.'

Salter looked again. Under the front of the cabin, in the gap between the supporting corner foundations, was a rock wall which had been taken apart and entirely rebuilt. They approached the cabin and Salter inspected the wall closely. One of the bottom boulders must have weighed a hundred pounds. 'How did you shift that?' Salter asked.

'With a crowbar.'

'And you lifted the others on? How long did it take you?'

'I started right after you left and finished about two o'clock.'

'Jesus Christ.'

But there was more to come. They walked round to the back door and Angus pointed up the slope to the outhouse. There was now a neat path through the brush four feet wide between the outhouse and the cabin.

'Jesus Christ,' Salter said again. He walked back to look at the rock wall with Angus following. He stared at Angus, who looked back, smug and smiling, sure of himself. He must have been working like a slave the whole day, Salter thought. Any second now we are going to do that scene where Pa Walton embraces John-Boy, both crying. We might even kiss.

'You can have that beer now,' he said.

*　　　*　　　*

They drove back in near silence. Angus, naturally, slept; Salter had trouble containing

277

the urge to sing.

Annie was waiting for them with soup and a hopeful look in her eye; the two men answered her questions over the shoulder while they unloaded the car.

'How was it?' she asked.

'Fine,' Salter said. 'I went fishing and Angus read eleven Maclean's magazines.'

'Didn't you go fishing, Angus?' she cried.

'I tried it. I didn't like it,' Angus said. The two men exchanged cheery looks.

'So what happened?'

'Nothing. I told you. I fished. He read.'

'Did you have a fight?'

'Fight? Us? What about?'

'Oh, bugger you,' she said, exasperated.

'We had a good time, didn't we, Angus?'

Angus giggled. 'Yeah. Never again, though.'

Salter laughed.

Annie looked from one to the other, understanding that she had got what she wanted. Later, when they stopped being male with each other, she could find out how it happened.